SPIT

RUTH SIBURT

Words Matter Publishing
P.O. Box 1190
Decatur, Il 62525
www.wordsmatterpublishing.com

ISBN 13: 978-1-958000-98-4

Library of Congress Catalog Card Number: 2023946307

Acknowledgments

Thank you, Richard, for teaching me what a story really requires. Thank you, Cousin Barb, for teaching me what perseverance is. I hope to join both of you on the other side. Thank you to my six siblings. Each of you, in your own way, showed me how important family is.

Dedication

Richard Peck my Mentor and
Barbara Mason my cousin.

Table of Contents

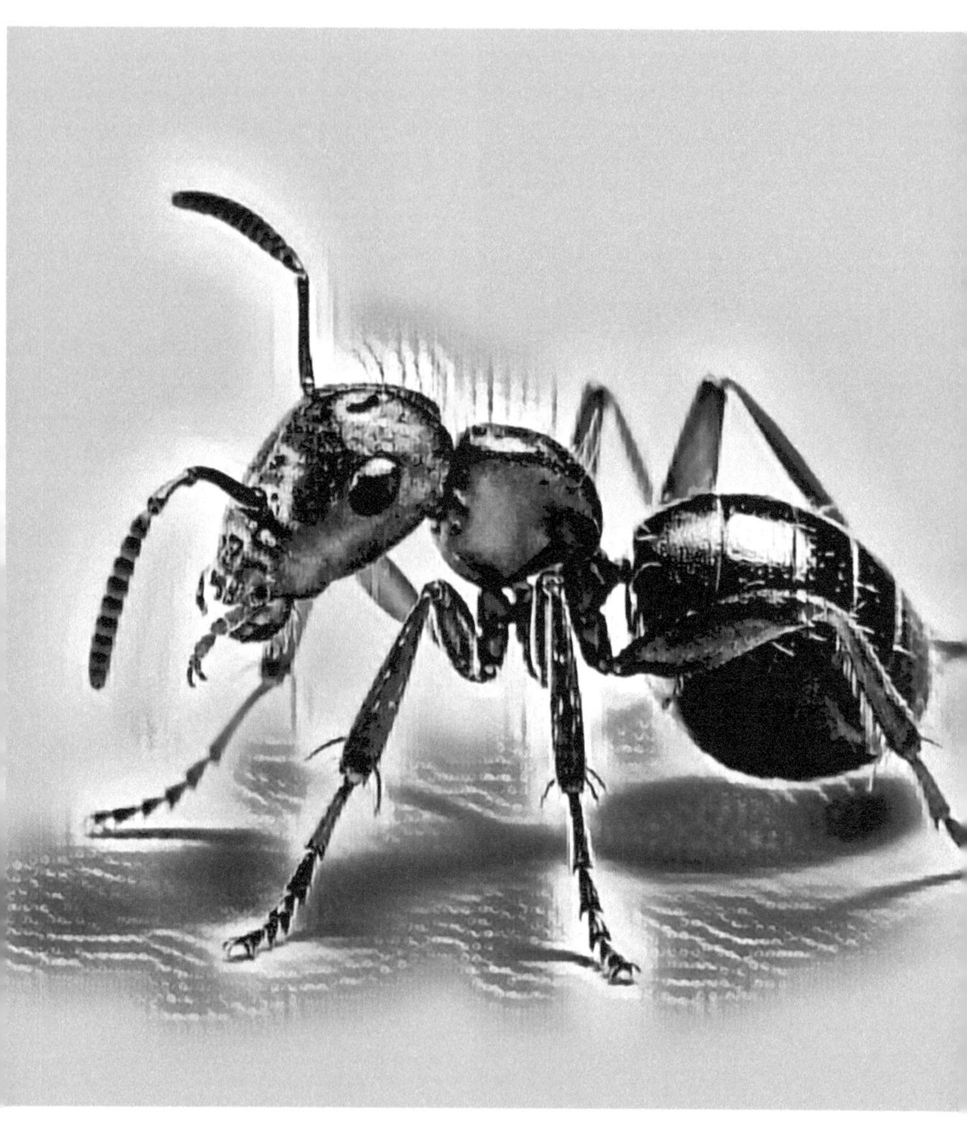

CHAPTER 1

Choosing Sides

JUNE 1963

My brother Cal is a wonder at spit. If the ant on my sneaker dared to cross Cal's foot, it'd be bug-history in the time it takes to hock a gob. I am not so hot.

Still, who knows? Today could be my day. I picture me, Jessica Louise Chrisman, hocking a stream of such velocity it sends this ant tail over teakettle into our side yard grass.

I tuck my chin and sight a line to my crooked right foot. I suck spit into the back of my throat. Suck, collect. Suck, collect. I trap a gob behind my front teeth. I breathe deeply. Purse my lips.

Splat!

The ant turns left and keeps on crawling.

I wipe the drool from my chin and look around, hoping no one saw. For once, I am in luck. All the players are watching Cal and Brody Beaman argue over who gets first pick for baseball.

"Tops don't count!" Brody yells.

"I notice they count when you're the one get'em," Cal says.

Cal and Brody are all-time captains in our neighborhood ball games. Brody is seventeen, two years older than Cal, a head taller, and twenty pounds heavier. But Cal's got Brody beat in the brains department; looks too, if you ask my best friend, Allie Hart.

"News flash," Brody says. "I ain't getting' stuck with your crip sister."

Cal's neck flushes red.

I look to the sky. *Please, God, don't let Brody pulverize Cal."*

"I'm not taking your stutter, buddy, either." Brody goes on.

I cut my eyes at Cal's friend, Eddie. He's toeing the dirt around second base. Eddie won't say a word about Brody calling him a name. It wouldn't do him much good. Eddie's speech is as twisted as my right foot. But Cal understands him, and Cal says there's nothing wrong with Eddie's brain. The two of them build stuff together all the time. I guess Cal should know.

Cal steps toward Brody. I glance at the sky again. *Please.*

"Brody, I can't figure out how come you're still in Stevenston?"

"Huh?"

"Charming as you are, I figured you'd be heading up President Kennedy's diplomatic corps."

Cal smacks the baseball hard in his glove. He points the glove at Eddie. "My best buddy, there's my first pick. And Jessie's my second."

Cal pops the ball again. "Go ahead now. You pick two."

Brody points his finger like a gun. "I'll take crashin' Kevin Fombelle, and Allie hurts 'em in the Heart: Stevenston, Illinois' base-stealing queen."

Allie pulls a face. She'd rather play ball for Cal, but she doesn't protest.

Allie is a year and a half older than me. When Allie grows up, she's going to be a famous singer like Brenda Lee. She'll have gorgeous gowns, hundreds of dollars, and a million fans screaming her name. Allie says she'll make me her backup singer.

I'm thinking about it. But I'd have to learn to carry a tune. And really, I'd rather be an astronaut like Valentina Tereshkova. She's Russia's first woman cosmonaut. President Kennedy is bound to let women into our space program now. We won't let the Russians beat us in Space. Besides, I told Allie, it's a cinch no one limps in zero gravity. Besides, I've never seen any cripple-footed singers. Allie thinks my foot won't matter. She says I hardly limp at all since my last surgery in St Louis. True, but I'm holding out for an astronaut.

There are three kids left to choose from: Sonny Kramer, Lindsey Barret, and Blinks Malloy. It's Cal's turn to pick.

"Blinks."

Oh boy! We're doomed for sure. Blinks wears eyeglasses as thick as canning jar bottoms. That's okay, except he doesn't wear them when we play baseball. Blinks claims the glasses throw his timing off. (As if Blinks ever had anything as fancy as timing.)

Brody takes our gorgeous neighbor Lindsey next. She'll be a senior this year. Lindsey has a night job. She's a carhop for Stevenston's Root Bear Deluxe. She's hardly ever awake in time for baseball. I'm pretty sure Brody has a crush on her.

That leaves Sonny to umpire. Sonny's face goes red. He might be blinking back tears. Sonny's twelve, like me. He's never had to umpire. Sonny's too good a player: strong and wiry and fast!

I trot my awkward trot over to Cal. "Why don't you take Sonny," I whisper, "and let me umpire?"

"Nope," Cal says. "I need you at first base."

Still, Cal sees Sonny's face.

"Hey, Brody, how about we call our own strikes and stuff so Sonny can play?"

Brody narrows his eyes: Suspicious. "Who gets Sonny?"

Cal turns the ball in his glove. "Let Sonny pick."

It flashes to me how this must feel to Sonny. It'd be like choosing between playing for the New York Yankees or the Three Stooges.

Sonny stares at the ground. He mumbles, "Brody."

Brody grins like he's been handed a hundred bucks.

I swallow a moan.

Cal nods and snugs his St. Louis Cardinals cap tighter.

Blinks shouts, "PLAY BALL!"

CHAPTER 2

In The Game

I snug my hand into my Uncle Joe's old glove and start for home base. Brody steps in front of me. "Where're you going, Crip?"

"It's five players against four." I protest. "We ought to get first bat."

"Nah. You had first pick." Brody shoulders his Louisville slugger. "First pick gets outfield. Rules are rules."

"First I ever heard you care about rules," I mumble.

I turn on my good left heel and trot over to first base. My muscles twitch. If I make just one good play today, I'll be happy. Trouble is, spitting isn't the only thing I stink at.

Brody steps up to the plate. Sonny hunkers down behind it, waiting for Cal's first pitch. Cal rears back and flings one low and away.

"That's a ball," Brody says.

"Hey! You can't call your own pitches!" I holler. "Let Lindsey call 'em."

Brody glares at me.

Lindsey steps up behind Sonny. "Ball one," She hollers.

Brody swings his bat low and level.

"Put one right here, Cal." He croons. "I'll send it smack into orbit."

Cal adjusts the bill of his Cardinal's cap. He leans back and lets the ball fly. It's a great pitch. Fast and slick, slicing through the summer air like Robin Hood's arrow.

Brody swings so hard he turns clear around.

"Ste-e-rike!" Lindsey calls.

"Huh!" Brody positions himself again.

Cal winds up and throws.

My mouth dries up. *CRACK!* Brody's bat connects. A blur of ball streaks straight for my head. I stick out my glove in self-defense. The ball stings my hand like a million hornets.

Brody stutter steps, thinking I've put him out. But the ball leaks out of my glove and thuds into the grass. Brody legs it for first.

I scramble for the ball. Lurch two steps off base. Scoop the ball up with my glove. I whirl around on my good leg. My crippled foot hooked around the good one.

Brody is just a step away.

I launch my body headfirst, glove out, toward first base.

Brody beats me.

"Safe!" he declares. "Safe! Safe! Safe!"

I roll over, squinting against the sun. Cal strolls to first. His shadow falls across my face. He reaches down. Pulls me to my feet.

"Sorry," I mumble.

"Nothin' to be sorry about." Cal flicks some dirt from my t-shirt. "Great hustle, little sister. Keep it up."

Cal trots back to the pitcher's mound. From second, Eddie flips me a thumbs up. At third, Blinks flashes a grin.

"Come on! Come on!" Brody complains.

Allie steps up to the plate.

Cal throws a strike.

Allie swings and misses.

"Keep your mind on the game, Allie," Brody yells. "Cal ain't gonna love you any less if you hit me in."

Allie gives her hips a twitch.

Cal throws another strike.

Allie hits a pop fly down the third baseline.

"I got it!" Blinks yells. He moves two steps to the left. Plants his feet. Braces his glove hand over his head.

The ball drops four feet to his left.

"So long, Crip!" Brody takes off for second base. Allie races for first.

"Get the ball, Blinks!" I holler. "It's right there!"

Eddie has one foot on second. His glove is ready for Blinks' throw. Blinks spies the ball. Scoops it up.

"Second!" Cal shouts from the mound.

Blinks, swivels, and flings the ball toward second base. But it is wide of the mark. Eddie makes a diving catch.

Brody slides into second. Eddie scrambles to his feet.

"G-g-great c-c-catch." Brody stands, slapping dust off his jeans. "T-t-too bad it d-d-on't count."

I can almost see steam rising from Eddie's ears. He turns his back on Brody. Fires the ball to Cal.

Crashing, Kevin Fombelle steps up to bat.

Cal throws two strikes.

Kevin watches them go by.

Kevin is a big redheaded kid. If Paul Bunyan had a kid instead of an ox, that kid would look just like Kevin. Now, with two strikes on him, I figure Kevin will swing at anything. I get ready.

Cal winds up. He throws a sweet curve that brushes the outside corner. Kevin lives up to his nickname. The ball sails miles over Cal's head and straight at Eddie. Eddie moves with the ball. He's back peddling so fast his cap falls off his head. The ball drops an inch from his outstretched glove. Eddie swoops down on it. Brody races for third base. Allie is already halfway to second.

Kevin is a crasher. But he's not much of a runner. Also, Keven likes to take a few slow steps to admire his hits. Cal covers second base, but Allie is only a step away.

"First, first!" I think. *"The only play is at first."* I plant my good foot on base and stretch out my crooked foot toward Eddie.

Eddie burns one at me. But it is a long way to throw, even for Eddie. It will be short. I adjust. Lean out as far as I can. My good foot goes with me. The ball whaps into the web of my glove. But I am off base. I whirl on my good foot. Stretch out so far, I fall face first in the dirt. I tag Kevin's leg as he slides in feet first.

"Out!" I scream.

Brody yells. "He was safe by a mile!"

"In your dreams!" Cal says. "Jessie got him fair and square."

"Reneging on calling our own outs, Cal?" Brody's fists double up.

"Nah, Brody. I ain't reneging." Cal spits a stream splat into the dirt. "Just figured you'd got better eyesight than Blinks, is all. Best let Sonny up to bat."

I toss the ball back to Cal.

Kevin parks one size twelve shoe on first base and one on the path leading to second.

Brody settles himself to catch.

I know Cal is mad from the set of his shoulders. I should be mad, too. But somehow, I'm not. I can still feel the sharp whap of the ball through my glove. The thrill of the whirling tag. I made the out. Whether it counted or not. I made it!

Sonny coils himself over home plate. He hugs that plate so tight even Sandy Koufax would have trouble finding Sonny's strike zone.

Cal throws one high and inside. Sonny must have felt the ball breeze by his chin.

"Ball one!" Lindsey calls.

Cal throws another inside and low this time. Lindsey thinks it caught a corner.

"Strike one."

Brody fires the ball back to Cal. "You hit him, Cal. He takes a base."

Cal turns toward second. Allie grins at Cal. Her right hip slung out to the side.

Cal squares around to the batter again.

Allie takes a two-step lead.

Watch her, Cal. I murmur.

I try to see everything at once. Cal throws the ball. Lights flash in my eyes. This is it: Sonny's pitch!

Sonny sees it, too. Of course, he does! Kevin sees it. Allie sees it and legs it for third, even before Sonny's swing clears the plate.

The crack of wood on ball sounds like lightning striking the ground.

Eddie races back.

If Sonny's power ball goes past the line of summer peonies, it is a home run, fair and square. But if Eddie can get to it before then…

Cal moves to cover home. I hobble fast as I can to split the distance between first and second base. The ball flies. Falls. Eddie launches himself toward the peonies. His arm outstretched. Everything is finally going toward the ball.

I swear I hear the ball bounce into his glove. Eddie rolls over once in the peonies. He jumps up showing the ball in his right hand.

"Eddie caught it!" Lindsey yells to her teammates. "Go back!!!"

Allie is only a step or two from home. She wheels and falls. She leaps to her feet and runs full out toward third.

I hurry- limp to second. Allie runs at me. Kevin tries to turn back to first.

I have two more steps to second base. One, limp, two, my good foot lands on the base. Eddie fires the ball. I stick out my glove. Whap! Allie is out!

"First, Jessie!" Cal hollers.

I turn on my bad heel and hurl the ball. It is a crazy off-balance throw. But I hear the snap in Cal's glove. Cal lays the glove against Kevin's leg as he slides in.

I can't believe it! Three outs at once! A triple play!

"Safe!" Brody hollers and prances around home plate. "Safe by a mile!"

Cal throws down his glove and starts toward Brody.

"No! Cal!" I scream.

Eddie runs past me. Fists clenched, pounding his way toward home plate.

Suddenly, Kevin is up. In two giant steps he is behind Cal. He pins Cal's arms. Lifts him right up off the ground.

"Nah, Brody. Cal got me. It's their bat." Kevin says and sets Cal loose. "One run to nothin. So far."

Brody acts like he's got more to say, but Kevin picks up his glove and strides out to second base. Allie, Lindsey, and Sonny head out to the field, too.

"Nice play, Jessie." Kevin tips me a wink. "What'd them St. Louis doctors do? Put some rocket fuel in your throwing arm while they were fixing your foot?"

I look down at my unmatched feet. I'm not certain how to take Kevin. But then I spy that same ant. Or maybe not. Maybe it's his ant-cousin. It doesn't matter. Hock, splat. Tail over teakettle it goes.

"Yeah, Kevin," I say, wiping spit from my chin. "Maybe they did."

CHAPTER 3

Chariots

Brody calls the game in the bottom of the third inning when we stooges take the lead. He claims he pulled a muscle and went hobbling off home. He mumbles how we better be watching for his old man if Brody can't work the garbage route with him tomorrow.

Brody's threats don't scare us. We aren't afraid of old man Beman, exactly. Least ways, not the same way Brody is.

Anyway, things fizzle out after that. Lindsey goes off to wash her hair. Kevin, Blinks, and Sonny figure they've got time to fish the lake off the community pier. Cal and Eddie naturally head on over to the garage and their homemade go-kart. Allie and me head for my house.

The first thing we notice as we step through the back door is the smell of chili bubbling in tomato sauce. Allie's eyes sort of glaze over. Both our stomachs are rumbling.

Allie whispers, "Jessie, see if I can eat with you."

I know what Allie has waiting at home: thin bologna and days-old bread. Plus, three younger half-sisters and a mom with a headache.

"Okay," I agree. "Wait here while I ask." Mom hates it when I ask for something in front of other people.

I open the kitchen door and leave Allie standing in the back entryway. What I see is even more heavenly than the smell. A pot of macaroni bubbles on the back burner. Chili Mac!!!! My favorite.

Mom looks up from stirring the chili. Her long brown hair held back by a leather barrette held in place by a wooden pic. She turns away from the stirring.

"What happened to the ballgame, Jessie?"

"We started winning, so Brody left."

Mom nods and uses a different long-handled spoon to stir the macaroni.

I say, "That sure smells good."

"Uh-huh. Who's waiting behind the door?"

"Allie. I kind of wonder if she could eat with us."

"You do, huh? What does her mom say?"

"It's great with her mom." We hadn't checked because it was likely Allie'd be stuck at home with her sisters."

Mom shoots me a look that means she knows I'm pulling her leg.

"All right then, you better let Allie in."

Allie lets herself in before I can turn the door knob.

"Thank you, Mrs. Chrisman!"

"You're welcome," Mom says and turns back to stirring. "But you two are going to have to work for your food."

"Sure, I love to cook!" Allie replies.

Mom clears her throat. "I've got that covered. But I need you two to set the table. I expect Cal and Eddie are tinkering with their old go-Kart. Eddie will need a place too. I expect you'd better set us six plates altogether."

"Absolutely, Mrs. Chrisman. We got it."

"Good deal," Mom says.

Allie and me take off for the dining room.

Mom calls after us, "First, Jessica Louise, change out of those flimsy sneakers and put on your real shoes. You hear me!?"

I hate my *Real Shoes*. "Yeah, I hear you."

"And wash your hands! Both of you!"

Allie follows me to my room. I toe off my ratty sneakers and shove my feet into the hated black and white oxfords. The right shoe is made especially strong. It has two extra layers of rubber on its soles. They try to make up the two inches shorter my right leg is to my left. The Oxfords help. But they're heavy and clunky.

We race to the bathroom and wash our hands. I make sure to pound my right Oxford hard across the floor so Mom knows I have the Oxfords on.

Allie and me take out plates and silverware from the dining room hutch.

"I'll do the silverware," Allie says. "You do the plates."

I set out six of our new plates. Mom gets a new plate for each $5 she spends at Gables Corner Grocery. The plates have blue and yellow stars criss/cross at the tops. I'm careful with the plates. I set them one by one around the table.

Allie places the spoon and knife on the right side of the plates and the fork on the left., "I think the knife and spoon are like husbands and wives. And the forks are their kids," she says. "That's why the fork goes all the way on the other side of the plate."

I figured if the fork stood for someone far off, it should be the dad. My dad is a trucker, so he's often far off. We still set his place at the table. Mom thinks on any day, he might surprise us early. Then we'd be glad he had his place set in the hope.

Cal and Eddie come in and wash up. Eddie's mom works an outside-of-the-home job. That means he gets lots of cool stuff. But it also means there's no one at his house making chili mac.

Eddie and Mom worked out a kind of sign language. Eddie rubs his hands together means this food sure looks good. And Mom says, "Thank you, Eddie."

He smiles big, which means, "You're welcome."

Mom passes the macaroni first and then the chili. Cal and Eddie pile it on like maybe they're astronauts ready for take-off and won't have anything but liquid food for days and days.

Mom passes the macaroni to Allie and me. "How's your mom getting along, Allie?"

"Pretty good," Allie replies, scooping macaroni onto her plate. "Except she's been throwing up a lot lately. She calls it the nine-month flu."

Mom's face flushes. "Well, I hope she gets better." Mom turns to the boys. "How's the go-kart coming along?"

Eddie's eyes shine with expectation. Cal speaks for them both. "Eddie says it's ready to go. We're ready to try it after lunch."

"Now, Cal, you know you're not to run that thing without your dad here."

"That was your idea!" Cal accuses.

Mom glares at him. "Your Dad should be home tonight. You can try it out tomorrow morning."

"What if he isn't home tonight?" Cal sulks. "Then what? Wait another week?"

Mom opens her mouth, but just then, a booming voice sounds from the open back door. "Anybody home!"

"Uncle Joe!" I scramble out of my seat and run to meet him. He scoops me up with one arm and swings me over his shoulder. My belly drapes across his shoulder, and my feet hang down his broad back. I lock my arms around his neck and breathe in the fine smell of him: Old Spice, machine oil, sunshine, and something special that is only Uncle Joe.

When he carted me around like this in St. Louis, all the nurses called him my chariot. They'd call, "Wish I had a chariot like your Uncle Joe?" That made Uncle Joe laugh. I felt like a Queen.

"Joe put her down!" Mom says.

Uncle Joe plops me in my chair.

Cal's eyes light up. "You busy today, Uncle Joe?"

"Can't say as I am.'

"Cal!" Mom warns, but with Uncle Joe around, we're in like Flynn.

"Eddie and me, we got this go-kart running, well almost, and Eddie figures…"

I stop listening.

I can almost smell the gasoline.

CHAPTER 4

Spark Plugs And Dinnerware

Uncle Joe walks around the go-kart, whistling low between his teeth.

"You boys do all this yourselves?"

"Pretty much," Cal says. "Eddie's dad gave us an old rider mower. We got the steering wheels and tires off that. The frame is from a water pipe, and the engine from a hunk-of-junk mower Grandpa gave Dad last year."

"Impressive!" Uncle Joe walks around the go-kart again. "Say you're having trouble getting the motor to turn over?"

"Yeah, but Eddie thinks maybe the spark plug needs adjusted."

"Sounds right. You got a feeler gauge?"

Eddie draws a silver ring from his pocket.

Uncle Joe nods, "That looks like a good fit."

There's a crashing sound from inside the house. Sounds like Mr. Gable will be getting a few more $5 worth of groceries.

Uncle Joe turns a half-smile toward the house. He hands the silver ring back to Eddie. "Go ahead. Give it a try."

Eddie kneels on the cement floor and turns the ring in his hands. Cal puts a wrench on the spark plug and twists. The plug comes free, and he hands it to Eddie. Eddie slides the metal ring between the body of the plug and an L-shaped piece of metal. He pushes gently on the metal, checks the ring, pushes, checks. He hands the plug back to Cal. Cal fits the plug back into place.

"That looks good to me." Uncle Joe says. "Fire her up."

Eddie slips into a used-to-be fishing boat seat of cracked green leather. He sits up straight with his right foot on a shiny silver pedal. He depresses the pedal-gives a circular hand signal. Cal puts a foot on the go-kart frame and grabs the pull rope. The engine vibrates itself to life. It sounds spluttery. Gray smoke scents the garage. Allie holds her nose. I think it smells fine—like rocket fuel. Maybe this is what Valentina smelled when she blasted off.

There's another crash from the house, but it's barely heard over the beautiful go-kart.

Pretty soon, the engine smooths out, and the smoke calms down.

Uncle Joe shouts above the noise. "Well, son, you gonna sit there or drive this buggy?"

Eddie leans forward, adjusts the steering wheel, and lets up on the brake. The wheels turn. We move out behind him in a knot.

Eddie steers the kart across our white-rock drive onto our side yard ballfield. He adjusts again, and away he goes around the baseball paths, past the peonies, around the garage, and across the white rock again. It is a bumpy ride. There's a grasshopper sticking to Eddie's t-shirt. But he doesn't notice. He's off on another round.

The third time he stops. Cal takes his place, and off he goes, I tug on Uncle Joe's hand. He bends down to hear me over the roar of the engine. "Can I drive it?"

"You'd better clear that with your mom."

"Huh-uh. She calls it a death trap. She'd never let me if I ask. But she'll listen to you."

Uncle Joe scratches his head. "I'm not exactly her number one pick on the hit parade, in case you haven't noticed."

"Please!"

Uncle Joe sighs. "I'll give it a try. But you have to promise if she turns us down, there'll be no crying."

"I swear. No crying."

Uncle Joe walks to the house.

Cal loops the peonies and lets out a war whoop.

Allie leans over to me. I'd almost forgotten she was there. "I wouldn't ride on that thing for all the tea in China unless Cal let me ride with him or Uncle Joe."

"He's not your uncle!"

"I know that," Allie says. "But he's a real dreamboat."

I roll my eyes, cross my fingers and wait.

Finally, the back door slams. Uncle Joe and Mom walk toward us. Mom is NOT happy! Her face is as angry as that Russian guy who hollered at that meeting.

Uncle Joe gives Mom a nudge. "Joe, you have gone right out of your mind!"

"Now, Mattie. You're going to love it! You wait and see." Uncle Joe flags Cal down on his next trip.

Cal pulls up. I watch how he stops the go-kart. He pushes in the pedal and moves the lever to the center. Uncle Joe bends over and tells Cal something in his ear. Carl jumps out of the seat.

Uncle Joe holds Mom's arm and pulls her toward the go-kart. Mom is still shaking her head, but she lets Uncle Joe push her into the seat. Cal leans in to give her instructions.

"Okay, Mom. Push in the pedal and move the lever down. Let out easy on the pedal, and away you go! To stop, push the pedal and move the lever back where it is now. See? It's simple."

Mom nods but twists around like she is getting out. Uncle Joe pushes down on her shoulders. "Come on, Mattie!" He shouts over the engine. "It'll be fun. You remember fun, don't you?"

She glares at Uncle Joe but works the pedal and moves the lever anyway. Just as the go-kart inches forward, Uncle Joe pulls the pick from Mom's barrette. Mom picks up speed. She wheels around the side yard, her long brown hair fluttering behind her.

Uncle Joe grins. Cal and Eddie grin. Allie fluffs her hair. I gape, open-mouthed.

Mom takes the peonies too sharp and smashes through them. She wrenches the steering wheel to the right and gets back on the path. The go-kart disappears behind the garage, then reappears. She bumps over the white rock drive and zooms past us again.

This time she clears the peonies. She rounds the garage again and eases the go-kart to a stop in front of us.

"Want a ride, Jessie?" Mom asks.

I can't believe my ears. "Sure!" I shout.

"Well, hop in. You'll fit just fine. I'll do the pedal. You work the lever."

I squeeze into the seat in front of Mom. Her arms and legs wrapped around me. I feel her heart pounding triple time against my back.

"Ready?" Mom asks.

"Blast Off!" I holler

I adjust the lever. Mom releases the pedal.

And away we fly!

CHAPTER 5

Diamonds

Everyone rides the go-kart, even Allie when Cal offers to take her. We ride so much Uncle Joe has to buy more gasoline. Best of all, Dad comes home before supper, and he drives it, too.

Now besides dirt base paths on the side lot, there are musheddown kart tracks everywhere. The greatest wonder of all is that Crazy Moon, who lives behind us, hasn't called the police on us for making so much noise.

Eddie goes home, but Uncle Joe and Allie stay for supper. I talked Mom into letting Allie sleepover. With Dad home, Mom is more likely to say yes to anything.

After supper, we sit on our front porch in the velvet summer evening. Dad lights a cigarette. The tip glows red. Despite the heat, Mom snuggles close under Dad's left arm. The porch swing sings a slow creaky tune with each gentle push.

Uncle Joe sits with Allie and me on the top porch step. Everyone speaks in low tones as if the night were a kind of church.

The grown-ups talk about grown-up things. Dad doesn't like how President Kennedy is pushing, pushing. First, the space race and now planning to integrate schools.

Uncle Joe pipes up. "Yeah, that space thing is crazy. Who on earth would care about crazy old space travel?" He gives my shoulder a friendly bump.

Allie and me get tired of the grown-up stuff. We beg mayonnaise jars from Mom so we can catch lightning bugs. Mom pokes air holes in the lids. We go deep into our yard, past the peonies, towards the Moons' backyard fence. The grass grows tall and ragged there. Lightning bugs rise out of the grass, blinking their silent signals to each other. We leap and dive, catching each tiny bug as if they are jewels. We trap them one by one, gently in our fists, and drop them into our jars.

We are careful not to raise our voices, not because of the night but because of Old Man Moon.

"Moon, Moon crazy as a loon." We chant at him in the daylight. He raises his fists and growls at us over the fence.

But everything is quiet now at Moon's house. My Grandpa Chrisman says Old Moon is a war hero. He got hit in the head with a bomb or something in the war. Not in World War II like Uncle Joe and President Kennedy, but in the Great War— the First World War. Dad says Moon is harmless. But he's scary anyway.

Moon's house is dark. But Allie and me keep quiet anyway, and we catch zillions of lightning bugs.

Allie touches my arm. "Shh, Jessie," she whispers.

"I wasn't saying anything."

"Shut up. I think I hear Moon."

I freeze. The lightning bugs wink on and off in our jars.

"I don't hear anything."

"Shhh! Listen."

This time I hear it: a trickle of water and a rustle beyond the chain fence. Then I see him. He's a shadow denser than the others in his yard. Except for the white of his face and hands and….

"Jumping willigers, Allie, he's taking a whiz!" I whisper a little too loud.

"Whose out there?" Moon calls. "Filthy Huns! Show yourselves!"

Allie and me race to the peonies. We crash down inside them, away from his crazy talk. We hold completely still until we hear him shuffle back to his house. His screen door screeches, then bangs shut.

"Wow!" Allie says. "That's the biggest one I've ever seen."

She's not talking about lightning bugs. "Don't be gross, okay?"

She shrugs her shoulders. "Let's make some rings."

Allie puts out her hand and captures a bug. "Got him."

She shakes it onto her palm and breaks off its golden body. She places the light on the third finger of her left hand. "I'm engaged," she croons. "Isn't my diamond magnificent?"

I capture another bug and open my hand. Its vinegary scent stings my nostrils. It crawls trustingly around my palm for a second or two, then takes flight.

Allie holds her hand in front of her face, admiring her ring.

"I believe you know my fiancé. His name is Joseph. He's quite tall, very big in manufacturing."

"What happened to Cal?"

"I gave him up years ago. He's only a boy, really. Joseph is a man."

"Well, I don't think Joseph is going to let you trot around the country singing."

"Of course he is. He understands completely. He'll hire a nanny for our children. Though we won't rush into that."

"You're cracked. You can't marry Uncle Joe! He's too old for you!"

"Well, he's a lot more likely to marry me than you! You can't marry your relative."

"I'm not going to marry anybody. Astronauts have no time for husbands!"

"Silly! That's because they're all guys."

"Oh yeah? How about Valentina?"

"Russian girls don't count. Anyway, she's engaged to that other cosmonaut guy. That's how she got into space." Allie says. "Besides, *American* girls can't go into space. *American* girls don't want to."

"A lot, you know!" I open my hand and fling my lightning bug away. It lands on Allie's blouse.

"Hey! What'd you do that for?"

I am flat mad at my friend. "You're the one who loves diamonds so much."

I twist the lid on my jar and shake all my bugs over Allie's head. Lightning bugs tumble onto her shoulders in her hair down the neck of her blouse.

"Get them off me!" Allie screams like I'd dumped scorpions on her instead of lightning bugs.

Grown-up feet come beating down the yard. Uncle Joe is the first to reach us. Allie throws herself at him. She wraps her arms around his waist and sobs against his chest.

Mom and Dad are close behind.

"What's going on here?" Mom demands.

"Umm, I kind of spilled my jar on her."

"Jessica Louise Chrisman!" Mom scolds. "That is the poorest excuse I've ever heard."

Dad sputters behind her. The end of his cigarette trembles in his mouth.

"Dan, please," Mom says. "This is not a laughing matter. Jessica Louise, you apologize to your friend!"

I am not sorry. Not one bit. But I manage to mumble, "Sorry, Allie."

"No harm done here." Uncle Joe unlatches Allies' arms. "You girls got to promise not to scream like that anymore. You'll give this old man a heart attack."

Allie giggles. Dad and Uncle Joe walk back to the porch.

"You girls listen to me," Mom says. "Any more *accidents,* and that will be the end of overnights for the both of you. Understand?"

We nod.

"All right then. Now let those bugs out of her jar. That's not a decent home for lightning bugs." Mom walks away, shaking her head.

Allie's still sniffling.

I pick up her jar and untwist the lid. I shake her lightning bugs on the peony bushes. They land in a sort of clump. They remind me of Christmas lights going off and on."

"Look, Allie, a Christmas tree."

Allie wipes her nose with the back of her hand. "Yeah, Christmas lights."

One by one, the lightning bugs take off zig-zagging into the night sky. Stars shine through wisps of clouds. I wonder what it is like in space. I wonder if an American girl will ever travel to the stars.

Allie stargazes, too. "Look, Jessie, so many stars. They sparkle like diamonds. Let's make a wish."

"We can't, now there's too many stars. That kind of wish only works with the *first* star you see."

"I don't care. I'm going to wish anyway." Allie crosses her fingers and shuts her eyes tight. "I wish, I wish." She opens her eyes. "Want to know what I wished?"

"NO!! If you tell, it can't come true."

"Okay."

"Want to know what I wish?"

Allie looks puzzled. "But then it won't come true."

"But my wish is my own true one." I say, "Not on a star."

"So, go ahead."

"I wish I hadn't dumped the lightning bugs on you."

Allie giggles. "That's okay." I wish I hadn't made you mad.

Allie spits on her right pinky finger. I do the same. We rub our spit-wet fingers together, hook them and pull.

"Friends forever."

We swear it.

CHAPTER 6

Relativity

"You get to choose your friends." my dad says. "And you make your own enemies. But you're just plain stuck with your relatives."

That's fine by me. Most of my relatives are great. Well, except Grandpa Chrisman's new wife, Lillian. She's always tsk-tsking over my crooked foot. Worse than that, her weird grandson Brett. He's eight and wears crazy clothes. He pretends to be whatever he's wearing. Last year he came as a bumble bee and said bzzz, bzzz, bzzz forever.

Other than those two people, I wouldn't trade families with anyone else. I wouldn't swap reunions, either.

The Chrisman Family Reunion is on the second Sunday in July at Mahomet, Illinois' Lake of the Woods. I have heard there are other Lakes of the Woods in other states, but I bet they aren't anywhere as fine as ours. There are rowboats and paddle boats, fishing, and hiking trails. Best of all, there's swimming at a beautiful sand beach.

Swimming is my best thing. Uncle Joe taught me when I was little. I can freestyle, dog paddle, breaststroke, and backstroke.

That's on top of the water. Underwater I can barrel roll, backward and forward somersault, and handstand.

In the water, I never limp.

Cal, me, Mom, and Dad all have our swimsuits rolled up in towels stowed alongside the picnic basket in the trunk of our car. This is strictly a Chrisman thing no friends allowed. So, Cal and me pick at each other in the backseat. I let my right leg stray over to his seat. He pinches my thigh.

"Ouch! Make Cal stop pinching me."

"Stay on your own side!" Cal counters.

Dad slows the car. "If you two can't behave, I'll turn this car around, and we'll skip this shindig altogether."

Now, if that had been Mom's threat, we'd go on picking. But Dad might really do it. He's not been so keen on the reunion since our real grandma died and Lillian stepped in.

We stop picking.

After about 122 hours of driving, we make it to Lake of the Woods. We tote our things up a hill to the pavilion Grandpa rents. Grandpa and Lillian and, of course, Brett wave to us. I let out a groan. But I am not surprised. Brett practically *lives* with Grandpa and Lillian. Lillian says Brett is "Creative."

Today Brett is wearing khaki shorts, a button-up shirt, and a pith helmet. He's running, heading straight for me.

He likes me. I don't know why.

Lillian calls out to him, "Take care not to hurt our Jessie. Poor thing."

Brett pays no mind and lands on my bad foot.

"Brett, for Cripe's sake!"

"Sorry, Jessie," he says. "But wait 'til you see what I found. This great log with all kinds of bugs and worms underneath it. Come on!" He's pulling on my hand.

"I can't go." I lie. "I have to help bring up our stuff."

"Go on with Brett," Mom says. "Cal can help."

I give Mom the evil eye. She smiles and waves us on.

Grandpa Chrisman crosses his eyes as we pass by. We can't help giggling.

Okay, maybe this time Brett might be fun. One thing is for sure he knows his directions. We step into the woods, and suddenly it is dark and cooler. Last year's leaves crunch underfoot. Gnats whirl in buzzy clouds. I shoo them out of my hair and wish I had a pith helmet, too.

"It's over here." Brett drags me to a gargantuan log.

"You never rolled that over!"

"No, but I rocked it a little. That's when I saw the bugs and stuff." Brett pulls my arm. "Come on. With the two of us, we're sure to turn it all the way over."

I sigh. At least Brett doesn't swim. I'll be shed of him then.

Brett and me fall to our knees beside each other. We brace our hands against the moldy bark.

"On the count of three," Brett says. We take deep breaths. "One, two, three!"

We push and push with all our might. But it doesn't budge. We slide down to rest beside it.

"There's gotta be a way." Brett's eyes fill with tears.

"Okay, okay, don't go all weepy." I hate when people cry. "Just let me think a minute."

I asked myself. "What would Uncle Joe do?" Well, probably he'd take out a crowbar, wedge it tight, and put all his might on the other end. We don't have a crowbar. But there are lots of fallen limbs. I send Brett on the hunting path for anything four inches around and four feet long.

In a few minutes, he was back, dragging two crooked limbs, one under each arm.

"Will these work?"

"Perfect! Give them to me." I poke Brett's in a spot. Then move a foot or so over to mine. We both put all our arm's length on the limbs.

"Okay, on my count of three. Bare down as much as you can."

Brett nods.

"One, two, three." We both put all our strength on our limb wedges. There's a loud crack, and I think Brett's limb must have broken, but no. It's the log. It moves! It does only two inches or so, but dang, if Brett isn't right. There are lots of things beneath that log.

He pulls a small magnifying glass from his pocket. We both drop to all fours. There are ants, of course, but other stuff, too, like slick-looking white worms, roly polys, red worms, and little green bugs.

Brett hands me the magnifier. I see a series of powdery-looking ridges. Some of them are broken open, and hundreds of pale bugs climb out of the cracks. It's so cool! Until I notice those pale bugs aren't moving anymore. Holy Cripes! It's an insect massacre!

"Push it back!"

"Huh?"

"They're dying! Don't you see that?"

"So?"

"So, I'm not a murderer. Get your limb. We're moving it back. NOW!"

"Okay! You don't have to yell."

We jump to the other side of the log and push our limbs until they should surely break. But they hold. The log slips back into place.

Brett is all flushed. "That was great! Wasn't it Jessie?"

The pavilion bell rings, and we race back.

Brett grins the whole way.

CHAPTER 7

Come And Get It

Mom gives me one look and reaches for a napkin. "Really, Jessie, how dirty can you get in just a few minutes? She dampens the napkin with a little spit and mops my face.

Grandpa Chrisman raises his hand for silence and pronounces the prayer. Mom stops scolding me.

The older folks go first. Then us younger ones. I look around for Uncle Joe, but he's nowhere in sight. Brett steps up behind me in the food line. I take one of Mom's chicken legs and a deviled egg. Brett takes exactly the same.

"Is that all you're eating?" Mom asks. "You still have to wait an hour before we swim."

I plop down beside Cal. His plate looks like he's recreating Mt. Everest. Brett squeezes in between us. Cripes, that kid bothers me. I take my first bite, then realize there's a sweet-sounding engine pulling up to the pavilion lot. Cal rubber necks it, then whistles high and clear.

"What?" I turn as well. It's our Uncle Joe in a beautiful blue convertible. The top is down, and his hair is blown every which way. Beside him is the most glamorous woman I've ever seen. She wears a silky pink scarf around her head. I think maybe she's a fashion model.

Suddenly, I don't feel like eating.

Uncle Joe hops out of the car, races to the other side, and opens her door. The woman rises from her seat like a princess.

Murmurs make the table rounds. Dad does an ear-splitting wolf whistle. Mom pokes him in the ribs.

"Everyone," Uncle Joe says. This is Kate." He turns to Kate with a sappy grin.

"Kate, this is everyone."

Grandpa Chrisman about busts a gut getting to them. "Joe, my boy, you sure know how to pick 'em." He bows low and kisses Kate's left hand. Grandpa startles and straightens. He flashes Kate's hand around. A diamond ring glitters on Kate's third finger.

Lillian hustles over. "Does this mean we have a date?"

"We're talking about a spring wedding in April, maybe. At the gazebo in Lyon's Park."

Grandpa claps Uncle Joe on the back. "Congratulations, boy!"

Kate smiles at Grandpa. She unwinds the pink scarf, and about twenty acres of honey-colored hair fall around her shoulders. A wave of Oooos echo through the pavilion.

Uncle Joe squires Kate around. He introduces her one by one to all the old folks. Then he picks up their plates and heads toward our table.

"Can I be excused?"

"May you?" Mom corrects. "If you're finished eating, yes."

I struggle out of the bench. Brett is hot on my heels.

Uncle Joe says, "Dan and Mattie. This is Kate. She's a nurse at County Hospital."

He says *nurse* like she's some kind of rocket scientist

Brett tugs on my arm. "Don't you want any cake, Jessie?

"No, I don't want any cake." I snap. "Quit following me around!"

Brett's face mooches in. "What are you so mad about?"

"I'm not mad. I just wish you'd leave me alone." I stomp over to the swings and plop myself in a curved rubber swing. Push off.

Brett rocks the swing next to mine. "Jessie, how come Uncle Joe's new lady has black around her eyes?"

"It's mascara," I grumble.

"Oh yeah, I forgot," Brett says. "Anyway, she sure is real pretty, isn't she, Jessie?"

"Actually, I think she's hideous."

"You do? How come?"

I almost say it. I almost tell Brett, the nurse-woman is stealing Uncle Joe from all of us. Instead, I say, "Never mind, Brett, it's none of our business."

I pump my feet like crazy. I've always wanted to fly my swing up and over the bar. I'd keep on flying over the treetops, past the clouds, all the way to the moon. There are probably no Kates on the moon.

Brett sits watching me. His head bobs like one of those stupid bobbing dogs in people's back windshields.

After a while, everyone is done eating. The women clear away dishes, and Grandpa tunes up his guitar. Now the old folks sing. Singing seems like an odd thing to do at a reunion, but they've done it ever since I can remember. Grandma had the best voice. Lillian, not so much. Anyway, they sing all kinds of songs. Grandma's favorite was the one about a frog that marries a mouse. She got a laugh out of that.

The good thing about reunion music is when it's over, we go swimming. I sit and swing and try not to think how close September suddenly seems. I try not to see how softly Uncle Joe's hand rests on Kate's shoulder.

The music lasts a pretty long time. Finally, Dad calls us to swim. I jump out of the swing at its arc. Brett drags his heels in the dirt, raising all kinds of dust. He trots after me.

"Where do you think you're going?"

"With you," Brett answers.

"No, you're not. You can't swim, remember?"

"Oh yes, I can. Grandma sent me to swim class. Now, I swim almost as good as you." Brett beams at me like this is good news. "Can I ride with you?"

"No!"

Kate must have heard him.

"You can ride with us, Brett." She smiles. "You come too, Jessie. Joe has gone on and on about you."

"No thanks." I think, *wish he'd gone on about you to me.*

"Jessie passing up a convertible ride?" Uncle Joe says. "How about you, Cal? Want to ride in Kate's chariot?"

"Sure!" Cal jumps into the back seat. Lillian hands Brett his towel and trunks. "Have a good time, but be careful. Not too far away from the shore, right?"

"Sure, Grandma." Brett climbs in beside Cal.

"Room for one more." Uncle Joe says.

"I don't want Mom and Dad to have to ride alone."

"That's my Jessie. Ever considerate of her parents."

Kate slides into the passenger seat, and Uncle Joe gets behind the steering wheel. They take off waving and shouting like Santa's elves in the Christmas Parade.

I climb into the back seat of our scroungy Ford. Wishing we had a top to put down.

CHAPTER 8

Deepwater

It's not far from the pavilion to the beach. We could walk it easy. But no one wants to walk after a few hours of swimming, so we drive.

I hurry into a dressing cubicle in the beach house. I rip off my shorts and top and pull on my red, white, and blue swimsuit. Mom and Kate are in cubicles next to each other. Their voices sound easy. Like they've known each other for ages.

I push back the curtain of my cubicle. "I'm going on out, Mom," I call

"All right," Mom says. "But don't swim beyond the buoys until we're there to watch."

I stuff my clothes inside a locker and race out to the beach. The sand is hot and burns my feet. I throw down my towel and quickly step into the water. I wade out waist-deep, then plunge beneath the surface face first. The water is green and clear, and it feels wonderful all over. Gurgling sounds fill my ears. My clever body pops me up to the surface. I float on top and watch for Mom to signal my freedom.

My family finally came out. They lay their towels together to sit by each other in the sun. Cal climbs the swirly slide first thing. He likes to plunge into the water the whole way first.

Brett stands with his toes at the lake's edge, testing the water, and shading his eyes. He calls, "Hey, Jessie! Want to see me swim?"

I ignore him. I raise my arm to Mom, and she waves back. Now I am free to swim across the buoys to the diving raft. I flip over onto my belly and do smooth, free strokes toward the raft. I pull the water toward me like a welcoming friend, just like Uncle Joe taught me.

At first, I am dodging bodies as I go. Past the buoys, the swimmers thin out. I bob my head out of the water. No one is between me and the raft.

If Kate wasn't here, Uncle Joe would be racing me to the raft shouting, *Last one on is a rotten egg.*

I reach the raft and pull myself onto the deck. There's a pair of sweethearts on the raft. They're kissing. He's rubbing her back with his hands.

I shake some of the water off and sit down on the raft to rest a bit.

"Hey, Kid," he says, "buzz off! We were here first."

But she doesn't like what he's saying. "Leave her alone, Mitch. She's not hurting anything. Besides, can't you see she's a cripple?"

"Doesn't mean she owns the raft!" Mitch says.

"Neither do you, Mitch." The girl stands up and dives into the water.

Mitch gives me a sour look and jumps in after her.

I stretch out on the raft, stomach down, facing away from the beach. The raft rocks a little. I imagine I am in a space capsule, and I've just dropped into the Atlantic Ocean. It's a pleasant wish-dream. In it, President Kennedy stands aboard a U.S. Naval ship that will bring me home. The president starts to take my hand. But then someone calls out, "Jessie! Hey Jess…"

It's Brett. I don't roll over. I am not interested. The President is waiting for my report.

There's another voice. A man's voice, loud and deep, calling from the shore. "*Brett! Brett! JESSIE, WAKE UP!*"

I turn over. There's a terrible commotion in the water about ten feet from the raft. Sandy white hair bobs up and down. The kid gasps with every bob.

Oh God! It's Brett!

I am out of a dream and into a nightmare. I jump up, shouting, "Brett! Reach out! Kick!" But he doesn't hear me. The water around him churns. Brett's mouth works like a fish. He gulps water, choking, spewing. For Cripes Sake!

I dive into the lake low and smooth. I kick hard, so I am only a few strokes away from Brett. I surface. I try to remember what Uncle Joe taught me about rescuing swimmers. How to hold them with one arm: how to kick from the side.

I reach the spot where Brett should be. I have to dive again because he is no longer bobbing. I dive again. Squinching my eyes, looking for the little idiot. I do a barrel roll looking, looking, and finally, there he is.

I hook an arm around his chest and kick us sideways toward the surface. Crazy Brett fights me. He claws at my arms and face. He's going to drown me, too.

I arch my back and kick again. I reach out with my right hand and pull the water toward us. My brain screams for oxygen. It says, *Let him go. Let him go.* But my left arm refuses. This is Brett. I will not let him go.

My lungs will surely burst. Suddenly, Brett stops struggling. He hangs limp in my arm. I aim my head like a bullet toward the surface. At last, I break through. I pull Brett's head and shoulders up with me. But now I am confused. Which way is the shore? Should I swim for the raft instead? If I choose the raft, how will I get him up there? I'll worry about that when I get there.

Brett hangs leaden in my arm. I have never been so tired. One stroke at a time, I whisper to myself. One more, one more. How far to the raft now? The water is my friend. No, the raft is my friend.

One more stroke. One more. Finally, the ladder is within reach. I hook my arm around a rough metal run. I hold on. I struggle to keep Brett's head level with mine. It isn't easy. He keeps slipping under the water.

"Wake up, Brett! Wake up! You have to help me!"

I can't hold on much longer. And I won't. In a minute, I'll let Brett go. But not right now. For just this long, never-ending minute, I can hold onto him.

Suddenly there is someone beside us. It's Uncle Joe. "Let him go, Jessie. I've got him." Brett's weight slips from my body. "That a girl. Now climb up on the raft."

Hands push me up and onto the raft. Kate follows me. Uncle Joe hands Brett to Kate. She rolls him onto his stomach and straddles his back. She pushes Brett's back and pulls his shoulders up, chanting under her breath.

I can't stop shivering.

Uncle Joe climbs onto the raft. He hugs them in his arms.

Kate goes on pushing, chanting, and praying.

Then finally, there is a beautiful belching sound. Green water and chicken skin burst from Brett's mouth. Brett chokes and sputters and pukes all over the raft. Kate pulls him at the waist, holding him out of the vomit.

"Atta boy, Brett!" Kate cheers.

A motorboat pulls up beside the raft. Men in orange life jackets take Brett from Kate's arms. They wrap him in a blanket. Kate steps into the boat and takes Brett in her arms again. Her eyes are ringed black like a raccoon's. Her honey-colored hair seemed styled in clumpy lake water. She is beautiful!

"Well, Jessie. It looks like you're the hero of the hour." Uncle Joe's hands clutch my shoulders. "So, what do you say? Shall we swim back to the beach or ride in this fine motorboat?"

I can't say anything. My teeth are chattering, and my legs shake.

"Huh! That's what I say, too. A hero always rides." Uncle Joe hands me to another of the life-vested men, who wraps me in a blanket, too.

Uncle Joe climbs in and takes me from the stranger. He holds me in his strong arms all the way back to shore.

He never once told me to stop crying.

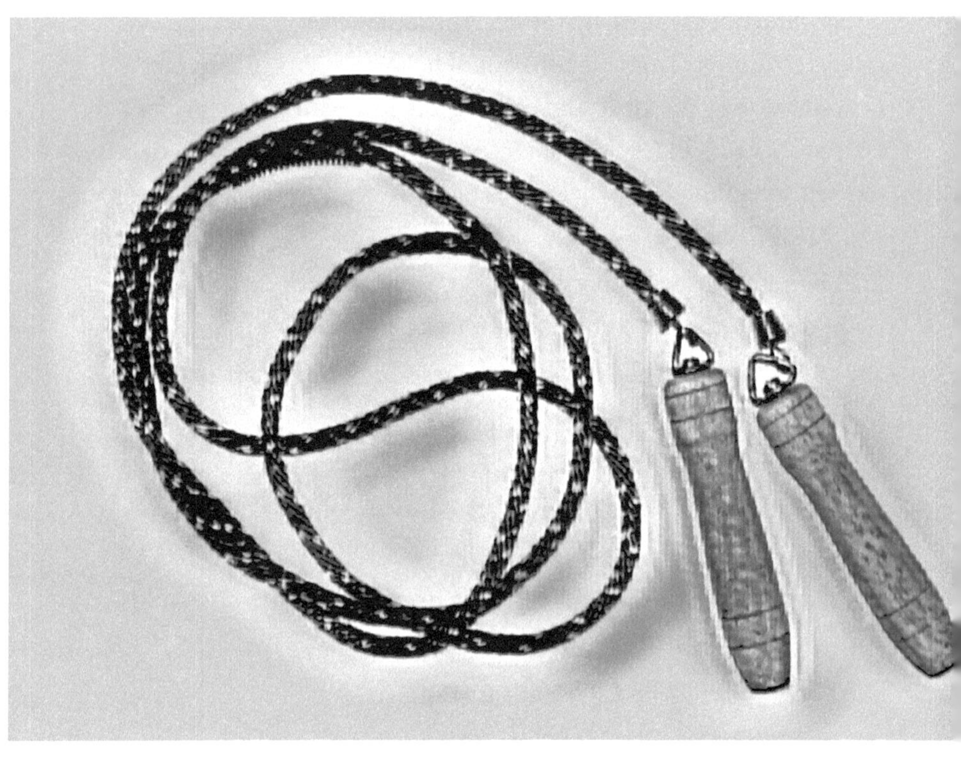

CHAPTER 9

Rope Songs

Allie's mom, Lacy, has raccoon eyes. She doesn't wear mascara like Kate, but her eyes look dark and smudgy as if she does.

My mom worries about Allie's mom. Having too many babies in a short time isn't good for a woman's body, Mom says. Lacy is pregnant again. Not huge pregnant yet, but showing. With Allie's stepdad changing jobs so much, Mom worries they might not have enough to eat.

Mom's garden is coming on, so she brings Lacy tomatoes, corn, and green beans. Food for the body. She also brings an armful of her most beautiful gladiolus, cream, red, and salmon-colored: beauty for the soul.

Lacy is delighted. She and Mom go inside to put away the vegetables and put the flowers in a tall vase.

Becca, Allie's seven-year-old half-sister, corners Allie and me. She wheedles us into turning rope for her. Becca plans to take Allie's place as Stevenston Elementary's jump rope champ this fall. Becca wants to be a winner, like Allie.

We start with Cinderella.

Cinderella

Allie won the title from third grade through sixth.

Dressed in yellow

But since Allie moved to junior high last year.

Went upstairs to

With Allie out of the way.

Kiss her fella

Becca has a chance.

How many kisses did she get?

We turn hot pepper for the kisses.
Becca misses after three jumps.
"You'll have to do better than that to be a champ," Allie says.
"You turned too fast!" Becca whines.
Allie rolls her eyes.
Allie looks like her mother, small and pretty and slim. Allie jumps rope like a dancer.
Becca looks like her father, Hank, tall and gangly. She jumps rope like an ostrich.
I guess they look so different because they have different fathers. Allie's dad went out for cigarettes one day when Allie was four. He must have had trouble finding his brand because he never came back.
"All right," Allie says, "we'll try Robbers. It's not so fast."
Not last night

But the night before

Allie's sisters all look like their father: too long for their bodies. It is almost as if, with Hank, Allie's mom has been erased. The only way to tell Lacy is still alive is if she keeps having babies. Lacy and Hank are trying for a boy, I guess.

Twenty-four Robbers
Came knocking at my door

They also fight. A lot.

As I ran out

Last winter, right after Allie's youngest sister Carla was born, Lacy and her four girls showed up on our porch late at night. Lacy's face was puffy and red. Her mouth was bleeding.

They ran in

Mom bundled all the girls into my bedroom. Allie cradled Carla and sang "Rock-a-bye Baby" to her, even though, as far as I could tell, Carla hadn't bothered to wake up.

Becca and Annie snuggled together like spoons and went to sleep on a pallet on the floor. Annie drooled all over the Bo-Peep pillowcase Grandma Chrisman embroidered for me.

Hit me over the head

Even with the door closed, I could hear Mom talking about phoning the police. But no policeman came. The next morning Hank showed up, blubbering promises. By noon everyone went back home. Everybody but Allie.

With a rolling pin

She stayed with me.

We turn hot peppers again for the lumps on Becca's head. This time she gets ten good jumps.

Allie says. "That's better, Becca. It might win in a second-grade competition."

Becca beams.

Lacy and Mom come out to watch us. They sit on the rickety porch swing and sip iced tea. Carla is asleep in the playpen. Annie makes mud-pie from spit and dust at the foot of the porch steps.

"I was pretty good at jump rope in my day," Lacy says.

"That must be where your girls get their talent," Mom says.

Becca asks for Teddy Bear next.

Teddy bear, teddy bear

Becca misses on the first trick.

Turn around

She can't turn around and jump at the same time.

Becca isn't ready to give up, "Let's do Fudge."

Fudge is not so hard.

Fudge, Fudge, call the judge

There are no hot peppers to mess Becca up

Mama had a newborn baby.
Wasn't a girl.

No spins

Wasn't a boy

No ground touches

> *Just an ordinary baby*
> *Wrap it up in tissue paper*

No running out and back in.

> *Throw it down the elevator*

All Becca has to do is stop the rope

> *First Floor*

At each floor.

STOP!

Becca misses. Her foot lands on top of the rope instead of catching it between her feet.

"Here, Becca," Lacy sets down her glass of iced tea and starts down the porch steps. "I'll show you how to do it."

"Lacy, do you really think you should?"

"Don't worry, Mattie. I won't jump hard."

Lacy stands beside the rope. Beneath the strings of her cut-off jeans, there's a fist-sized purple bruise.

"Okay, girls, start turning," she says.

We sing,

> *Fudge, fudge*
> *Call the judge*
> *Mama had a newborn…*

But Lacy has stopped jumping. She is bent over, holding her belly, and trying to breathe.

Mom runs off the porch. She wraps her arms around Lacy and helps Lacy up the porch steps. Mom eases Lacy onto the swing.

Lacy chants, "I'm okay, I'm okay."

But even I can see she isn't.

"Jessie, you and Allie take the girls to our house. Look after them. I'll be along soon."

I start up the porch steps trying not to see the bright spots of blood on them. I pick up Carla from her playpen. She murmurs a little but doesn't wake. I pick up the bottle. Allie, Becca, Annie, baby Carla, and me go home to wait.

At home, we put baby Carla on my bed. She hardly moves. We surround her with pillows so she won't fall off.

I make everybody peanut butter and jelly sandwiches and pop some popcorn. It almost seems like a party.

Except it isn't.

After lunch, we try to play Monopoly. But Annie is too young to know about money. She can't even count the dice yet. Then Carla wakes up, and we put it all away. We wouldn't want Carla to choke on the top hat or the little iron shoe.

I wash out Carla's bottle with steamy hot water and refill it with fresh milk. Allie feeds her. She wiggles around in Allie's arms until she finds a familiar spot to rest in.

It's hours before Mom comes home. Just when I begin to worry about what I can make for everyone's supper, Mom is there.Allie asks, "Is my mom okay?"

"She'll be fine, Allie." Mom sets a paper sack full of the girls' clothes on our coffee table.

"But she needs to stay in the hospital for a night or two. She says you girls can stay with us tonight."

"The baby?" Allie's voice is so low I can hardly hear her.

Mom shakes her head. "I'm sorry, Allie."

Carla finishes her bottle and wiggles down from Allie's lap. Carla is learning to walk. She takes tottering steps, holding onto our living room sofa. She falls, plop on her butt—whimpers—gets up again. Allie goes to her baby sister and offers her two fingers for each hand. Carla smiles and grabs hold. Now Carla can go anywhere she pleases. Shuffling along like a little old lady with humped-up shoulders, Allie steadies each tiny baby step.

CHAPTER 10

The Fair

Since Allie's mom lost her baby, it's like Allie is glued to her. She hardly ever comes over.

It's weird Allie's mom losing her baby on practically the same day President Kennedy's baby died. Everybody was so sad for little Patrick Kennedy.

Lillian says it's probably for the best. Probably something was wrong with the babies, both Jackie Kennedy's and Lacy's. Lillian says the Kennedys wouldn't want a crippled child, and Lacy can't afford one. She says it's God's will.

Mom says God grieves for the babies, too. They were His babies as much as they were Jackie's or Lacy's.

I don't know about all that. I only know that since it happened, Allie hasn't played one inning of baseball or stayed the night with me. Worst of all, Allie won't come to the fair. Not the junky old county fair either, but the Ringling Brothers, Barnum and Bailey, Maximum Overdrive State Fair way over in Springfield. I can't believe she's passing up the chance. I wouldn't. Not in a zillion, skillion years!

Cal, Eddie, and me are going with Lindsey in her cherry red 1953 Chevrolet with the white hard top, the radio, and the miniature pink ballet slippers hanging from the rear-view mirror. I can't believe it!

I almost didn't get to go. I almost got stuck at home shucking corn with Mom instead of sucking down corn dogs. And the reason I almost didn't get to go? M-O-N-E-Y!

It seems like all Cal has to do is bend his pinky finger, and people pay him. He gets $5 for mowing the yard and a buck every time he hauls groceries over to Crazy Moon's wife. So, Cal is rolling in dough.

I'm a different story. Washing dishes doesn't count, hanging out clothes doesn't count, and even helping Allie's mom with her babies doesn't count for money. I'm supposed to be *happy* I can help out, not expect money for my work.

Dad tried to come through for me. He wants to build a barbecue pit in our yard, so he got a bunch of these crummy, free bricks from some guy. I clean the mortar off the bricks at a penny a brick. It takes three hours to earn a quarter that way. The mortar burns my fingers, and the hammer is rough on my knuckles when I miss the chisel.

Things were not looking good for my first trip to the State Fair. Because Mom said I had to have my own money if I went, not depend on Cal, Eddie, or Lindsey.

Then, just when everything looked hopeless, who, of all people in the wide, wonderful world, should come through for me? Lillian! She sent me a card and $10, thanking me for rescuing Brett. That's fate!

Mom makes me put $1 in my savings account. And I have to save fifty cents for the offering plate. But that still leaves me $8.50 plus the .50 cents I earned cleaning bricks for Dad—more than enough to go to the fair.

So, here we all are Lindsey, Cal, Eddie, and me tooling west on Route 36 at about 60 miles per hour in Lindsey's Chevy. We've got every window cranked down, and the wind roars around us like a madman.

Lindsey's hair whips all over her head. Her radio is cranked up to the beat of some golden oldies. Cal's rapping on the dashboard with his fingers. Eddie's bopping in the back seat, singing under his breath. I'm twisting in my seat, like maybe I'm going to be invited to the next television dance show. I am much better on my butt than on my feet.

We've been driving for almost an hour, and we're getting really close to Springfield. There're signs all along the way. That makes me feel better. I hate strange cities. I'm afraid of getting lost. But the other three have been here before, so it should be okay.

Lindsey slows the car, and the wind is not so wild.

We wind around the unfamiliar streets. I'm surprised to see Springfield looks a lot like Stevenston: some nice houses, some crummy ones, railroad tracks, auto-salvage yards, and barbershops. Somehow, I expected a Capital City to be different.

"I hope you can find the fairgrounds because I've never approached them from this direction," Cal grumbles.

Lindsey laughs. "Just watch for the signs."

Eddie and me peer out our windows, looking for fairground signs. It isn't long before we see one. Lindsey turns and follows it.

The signs are closer together now. Even so, the fairgrounds spring on us out of nowhere. But there is no place to park nearby. Lindsey turns a corner and searches the lots people have made in their yards. At last, four blocks from the main entrance, there is a yard with a space. A boy about Cal's age waves to her with his pennant. Lindsey turns into the yard.

"Got one space left," the kid leans in through Lindsey's open window. "It'll cost you one dollar to park."

"A dollar!" Cal bristles. He is a born bargainer.

The kid pushes his head into the car. He's checking out Lindsey's legs.

"$1," he says.

"The closest lots only cost .50 cents," Cal says. "You're four blocks away."

The kid shrugs, "Whyn't you park up there then?"

"Come on, Cal, that's .25 cents apiece. Here's mine." I dig one of Dad's quarters out of my jeans' pocket and plunk it into the kid's hand. The others do the same.

The kid grins and backs out of Lindsey's window. Lindsey parks on the ruined grass. We get out, and the kid waves to us, flipping one of our quarters into the summer air.

Cal and Lindsey lead out. Eddie and me bring up the rear. Eddie maneuvers himself to the outside of the sidewalk between me and the traffic. Cal does the same with Lindsey.

I think, hey, what gives?

"The perfect gentleman," Lindsey says. Cal crooks his arm. Lindsey tucks her hand in the bend of his elbow.

They're clowning around, I think. But I'm pretty sure I'm not going to tell Allie about this part.

Eddie grins at me. For a minute, I think he might offer me his arm, too, but he doesn't. Thank Goodness!

The sidewalks are crowded. We hear the fair's bright, tinny music while we're still a block away. Barkers call through bullhorn speakers, and shrieks of laughter echo from the rides.

We pay our entrance fee and push through the turnstiles. The sounds that drifted over us on the street outside the gates are so loud inside I feel surrounded: smothered by a blanket of noise. We have to shout to be heard, even though we are standing next to each other.

The smells are almost as overpowering as the noise: oily corn dogs and elephant ears, buttery popcorn, sizzling peppers, dust, sweat, animals, and straw. Overhead, people dangle their feet from open metal chairs, which slip and jerk along thick cables.

"There, that's what we should do first," Lindsey points to the overhead chairs. "We could figure out where everything is."

Cal seems to consider it. "Nah, let's walk around for a while first. Save that for last."

A shrill whistle sounds from above us, followed by a booming voice. "Hey, look. Somebody let the freaks outta the tent."

We look up in time to see Brody leaning over the bar of one of the overhead cars. He is with somebody I've never seen before, but judging from the condition of the other kid's acne, I'm sure it's a Beaman relative. Brody is on the upward swoop of the cable. He tips a paper cup, and yellow liquid spills out. It misses us by inches.

"Beer? How did Brody get beer?" Lindsey wonders.

"Probably Brody's old man got it for him," Cal says.

"Well, forget what I said about the sky ride. We might get Brody's seat and catch a galloping case of the stupids," Lindsey says.

We walk along the main paths, weaving in and out of lines of people waiting for food. It has been a long, hot ride, and we are thirsty. We join a line waiting for lemon shake-ups. I can't believe the price of things. I peel off another dollar from my tiny roll and get back fifty cents and a drink that's mostly ice. At this rate, I will be broke by noon. But the drink is wonderful: sweet and tart and freezing on the throat.

We stroll and sip and consider what to do first.

"Test your skill," the barker cries. "Five shots for a dollar. Win the pretty young ladies a teddy bear."

"Ride the amazing 'Loop d' loop.' Defy the laws of gravity."

We buy four tickets to the "Tilt-a-Whirl" and jam ourselves into the same dish. Cal and Eddie take the outside with Lindsey and me between them. The "Tilt-a-Whirl" music begins. The dishes rotate on their tracks, spinning us round and round, raising and lowering slowly at first, then faster and faster until the centrifugal force sends us crashing into each other. The world outside becomes a giant kaleidoscope.

When the ride stops, we get out and crash into each other. Our balance is shot. It only lasts for a minute or two. When we can walk straight again, we head for the "Loop d' loop" roller coaster.

Only two people are allowed in the car on this ride. Cal and Lindsey take the first car. Eddie and me take the second. Cal and Lindsey sit so close their shoulders are touching. Eddie and me have inches to spare. There's no music on the roller coaster. The cars travel so fast that I doubt music could keep up.

Straight up we go, then plunge down. We all throw our hands over our heads on the descent, proving how brave we are, screaming the whole way. Whip! We veer right. I slam into Eddie. Everything is wild and fast. We loop the loop, and the ground rushes up to meet us. At the last second, the car levels out again.

We stagger out with our blood high in our cheeks. We rush to the next thing. The double Ferris wheel. Then the mile-high slide.

Lindsey wants to ride the carousel, but Cal balks. So, Lindsey and me go alone. Cal and Eddie cross the path to the duck shoot.

We run to the sweet music. Painted horses slide up and down on golden poles. I choose a gleaming black stallion with a silver bridle. Lindsey picks a dashing white. The music swirls around us. Mothers steady their children in their saddles. Sweethearts trade up-and-down kisses.

Across the way, Eddie sites down the barrel of an air rifle. Cal watches Lindsey and me ride round and round in three-quarter time. I hear the duck-shoot barker call out, "Bulls-eye!" My amazing black stallion sweeps me away on another round.

Too soon, the carousel stops. We walk back through the gate. Cal has a pink stuffed poodle tucked under his arm. He holds it out for Lindsey.

"You won this?" She asks.

Cal hunches his shoulders.

"Thanks." Lindsey cradles the dog against her chest.

Sheesh, you'd think that stupid dog was the Hope diamond or something.

"Let's eat," I say.

We walk back the way we came. Back to the little aluminum trailers selling corn dogs and sausages. We each get a corn dog and a Coke. Eddie buys us some river fries to share. We find the one scraggly tree that no one else will claim and sit down in its ragged shade to eat.

The corn dogs are fresh and hot. I have to bite into mine gently in order not to burn my mouth. The clock on the outside of the exhibition building says it is 3 o'clock. We promised Mom we'd be home before 6. We are running out of time.

CHAPTER 11

Art And Fortunes

After lunch, Lindsey and me drag the guys through the arts and crafts building. Cal and Eddie groan, but we take our time.

Lindsey likes the sculptures. I wander along the youth art competition. There's this great oil painting entitled "Reaching the Moon!" It shows a silver rocket ship slicing through inky dark space. There's no ribbon on this one, but if it was up to me, it would win the whole shebang.

Eddie looks over my shoulder. He taps my arm, points to the picture, then to himself, and launches a leveled hand skyward, drawing flight as surely as the artist of the painting has.

"You want to fly to the stars, too?" I ask.

Eddie nods.

Cal and Lindsey come up behind us.

"I've had all the culture I can stand," Cal says. "Let's go back to the rides."

We walk back to the main track. I have only enough money for another ride or two.

We walk past the "Tunnel of Love."

Lindsey leans over and whispers to Cal. Cal blushes. He turns to Eddie and me.

"Umm, how about this ride?"

Eddie and me stare at him.

Cal's face goes redder. "Come on, you guys, I mean it."

"Have you gone bat crap?"

"Don't cuss. I'll tell Mom."

"Sure, right after you tell her you went through 'Tunnel of Love' with Lindsey."

"Well, Lindsey and me are going. You and Eddie can come or not."

"Eddie and me wouldn't be caught *dead* in that hokey place. So, go ahead by yourselves!"

"Fine," Cal says. Off they go to get in line.

Eddie and me watch them. But Lindsey and Cal don't look back. She's still holding that dopey dog, and Cal is standing so close to her he blocks her shadow.

"What do you want to do?"

Eddie hunches his shoulders.

We start back to a drink wagon. On the way, we pass an army tent with multi-colored streamers flying from its poles.

"Fortunes by Madam Magda, $1," a hand-painted sign declares.

Eddie stops outside and points. Do I want to do that?

"Sure, that'd be great. But if I do that, I won't have enough for a drink."

Eddie pats his chest. The fortuneteller is his treat. Eddie lifts the tent flap, and we step inside. It's musty and dark.

A bushy-haired woman sits at a round table covered with a checkered cloth. Her teeth are bucked, and her lips won't close over them. There's a crystal ball on the table that looks like the gazing globe Lillian has in her puny flower garden.

"Who wishes to consult Madam Magda?" She says, flattening out her vowel sounds, like my cousins from Chicago.

"I didn't know there were gypsies from Chicago," I say.

"Fortune telling is a gift," she says, "not a nationality. Who is first?"

Eddie digs in his pocket and plunks down two one-dollar bills on her cloth. Madam Magda scoops them up and shoves them down the front of her blouse.

"Give me your hand," she says to Eddie.

"Aren't you going to use your crystal ball?" I ask.

"No, the crystal ball is for old people whose lines are hard to read."

"I don't see why old people's lines should be any harder than young ones," I say.

Eddie gives her his hand. Madam Magda turns it palm up. She traces the lines inside it with her index finger.

"I see much pain here," she says. "Many difficulties with speaking."

There's nothing psychic about that. Eddie hasn't made a sound since we entered the tent.

"I also see a clever mind and a valiant heart. You are brave and generous."

I think it sounds like she's reciting the Boy Scout oath.

"You will have a good life. And a long one. I see conflict in your immediate future. Be forewarned. Stand your ground. Assistance comes from an unexpected source."

Eddie nods. His fortune is told. He rises, smiling at me, and motions me into his chair.

I don't believe a word, Madam Magda says. I figure we could have got as good of a reading out of a Bazooka Bubble Gum package. But Eddie has paid my way. The least I can do is let her read. I put my hand, palm up, into hers.

Madam Magda's eyes my oxfords. Her fingers trace through the lines. "You, too, have had much pain."

"Not so much," I say.

Madam Magda drops my hand. "Do not interrupt, or a reading will be impossible."

Sheesh, who'd think Chicago gypsies would be so touchy? "Okay, sorry."

She picks up my hand again.

"Your strong will brings you many blessings but also causes you conflict." Madam Magda says. "Your greatest strength is in your weakness."

I open my mouth to protest this double talk, but Eddie pokes me with his finger, and I keep still.

"Hold fast to your dreams." Madam Magda drops my hand. "You may blaze a trail others will travel. You must aim for the stars to land in the clouds."

"What? That's it? How about my life? Will it be long and good? Will I get what I want?"

"A better question is will you want what you get?"

"Well, if that's not the worst fortune I ever heard. You should give us our money back."

"There are no refunds in the future." Madam Magda spreads her hands and shews us from the tent.

"What a crock! Let's get a drink."

We take two steps then something hard slams my back. My breath explodes in my lungs. I stumble, and Eddie catches me.

"Well, if it ain't the crip and the stutter-buddy," Brody calls from behind us. My stomach sinks into my oxfords.

I look around for Cal and Lindsey. Brody likes Lindsey. He'd never really hurt us if she was around. If Cal were here to back Eddie up, Brody would think twice, too. But with only Eddie and me, we're in for it.

Brody has a half-full cup of beer. I'm busy calculating the chances of Eddie and me making a run for it. Eddie could outrun Brody for sure, but I'm a different story.

Brody picks up another clod. It looks like a piece of pavement. Eddie whispers in my ear. I think he's saying, "Stand here."

Eddie takes five steps away from me. He gives Brody the middle finger salute. Brody's face turns tomato red. He throws down the beer, and the pavement clump. He lowers his head and charges like a rabid bull.

Brody pounds only inches away from me with murder in his eyes. Out shoots my crippled foot. Brody lurches headlong on the path. Gravel skitters away from his hurling body. Blood runs from his nose, and his forehead is raw. He swears like a sailor and blubbers like a 3-year-old.

Eddie takes a handkerchief from his pocket and hands it to Brody's buddy.

"Look at what you did. His old man ain't gonna be happy about this."

Eddie points to himself and shakes his head. He busts a gut laughing. Points to Brody, then to me. It's clear what's got Eddie so tickled. The great Brody Beaman was reduced to a bloody, sniveling beer puddle by a GIRL!

Brody and his buddy have got nothing else to say. Some grown-ups in white uniforms with red and blue first aid patches hotfoot it in our direction. Eddie motions for me to follow. We go in search of drinks.

When we get to the drink wagon, Eddie won't let me buy. I choose lemonade, hoping it will calm my stomach.

It seems like half my life, I've been wishing someone'd deck Brody Beaman. I never in a zillion years figured it'd be me. I should feel like Superman or at least Nancy Drew; mostly, what I feel like is puking.

Eddie raises his paper cup and bumps it against mine. A toast. He says I'm either "brave" or "crazy." I can't make out which.

I think maybe it doesn't matter.

Maybe when it comes down to it, crazy and brave look exactly the same.

CHAPTER 12

A Face At The Window

State fair time is only a hop, skip, and jump away from my birthday!

If I had known Dad wanted all those bricks cleaned so he'd have the barbecue pit built in time for my birthday cookout: I'd have complained less and worked harder. We finished in time, barely.

On the Thursday before my birthday bash on Saturday, I climbed onto an overturned five-gallon bucket to set the last brick. Uncle Joe named it the Jessica Louise Chrisman Honorary Barbecue Pit. It looks a lot like the Old Woman's Shoe from the nursery rhyme. I reckon it'll cook hotdogs, okay.

Mom invited pretty much everyone we know. She says turning thirteen is a really big deal. Like I'm sticking my big toe into adult territory. I'm not crazy about it myself. The best part of turning thirteen is Allie and me are only a year and a half apart in age.

Grandpa, Lillian, and Brett are the first to arrive. I haven't seen them since the reunion. I worried drowning might have hurt Brett's brain. He's the first to jump out of the car. I see right away he's the same old Brett.

Today he wears one of Lillian's white blazers. It reaches almost to his ankles. He's looking through a pair of Grandpa's cracked reading glasses.

"Hello, young woman." He sticks out his hand and grabs mine. "I'm Albert Schweitzer. Glad to make your acquaintance."

"Hello, Al."

"E equals MC squared."

I don't mention he has his Alberts mixed up.

Allie arrives next, and for once, she is without her troop of little sisters. She hands me a flat package wrapped in gold paper with an enormous white bow.

"Want to see if you can stay the night?"

"I don't know, Jessie. Mom is still pretty weak."

"Come on. It's been *weeks* since you stayed over."

Allie shrugs. "Maybe. I'll call later and ask."

We take Allie's present over to the card table Mom set up in the yard. She put an old linen tablecloth over it in dyed pink to try to cover the brown gravy stains. That worked pretty well. I put Allie's present over the darkest spot so no one will ever know the cloth isn't perfect.

People arrive in clumps. Uncle Joe and Kate. Cal walks across the yard to escort Lindsey over.

Dad calls Cal and Lindsey the book ends because you hardly ever see one without the other anymore. I know Allie has to notice, but she isn't saying anything.

Eddie, Blinks, Kevin, and Sonny come.

The gift table looks overloaded. I am itching to tear into the presents.

Mom organizes the games. They're all silly games, the same ones we play every year. But even the grown-ups play them.

Uncle Joe's favorite game is the water relay, where we choose teams and try to fill a pint jar with tablespoons of water carried from a bucket. Uncle Joe and me are always on the same team, and we always beat the pants off our competition. Even if we don't beat them, he always *thinks* we beat them, which is almost as good.

Everything is going great. Dad burns the hotdogs black, which is exactly the way I like them. Mom made a tremendous sheet cake and wrote "Happy Birthday, Jessie" and a huge "13" in red across the center. We had watermelons icing down in coolers since yesterday, and they are sweet and juicy—the best anyone has tasted this year.

When Dad lights the thirteen candles plus one for luck, and everyone sings "Happy Birthday, Dear Jessie," I don't want to blow out the candles at all.

I want to go on watching them flicker in the wind. I want to hold on to the feeling I have this instant. This could be the absolute best moment of my life, and I don't want to step past it. Ever! But Uncle Joe is watching me, and Kate, and Mom and Dad, Eddie and Allie.

"Blow out your candles, Jessie, and make a wish," Dad urges.

"I wish I never had to blow them out," I say.

Everyone laughs.

"I wish. . ." I begin.

"Not out loud, Jessie. You can't say your wish out loud." Brett reminds me. "Those kinds *never* come true."

"All right." I close my eyes and wish for the next best thing. I wish for everyone to be exactly as they are in this instant, forever.

"All right, already," Cal says. "Make your wish before the cake melts."

I open my eyes and take in the biggest breath I can. I blow and blow. All the candles go out, except for the one that's for good luck.

"Aw," Brett says, "too bad. Now you won't get your wish."

"Of course, she will, Dr. Schweitzer," Uncle Joe says. "Everybody knows the good luck candle isn't a wishing candle."

And now I get to open the gifts.

I think I will never have a better birthday if I live to be 1,000.

Eddie bought me a tiny gold heart on a fine chain. Allie gave me her best Brenda Lee album. Lindsey gave me a snow globe with the Illinois state capitol building inside. Uncle Joe gave me a brand-new ball glove. Mom and Dad gave me patent-leather red shoes. Lillian gave me another $10 and two sets of baby doll pajamas. Brett gave me his magnifying glass, which was only slightly scratched. Best of all, Kate gave me a make-it-yourself model of Friendship 7.

After the gifts are opened, the party winds down. Grandpa and Lillian leave and take Brett with them. Sonny and Kevin, and Blinks leave together just like they came. Cal and Lindsey stroll off into the sunset. Eddie leaves a little after that. The others drift away too, everyone calling "thanks for the party" to Mom and "Happy Birthday" to me. Pretty soon, it was only Mom and Dad, Uncle Joe and Kate, and Allie and me left.

Mom says Allie may sleep over. Allie's mom says the same. And Allie needn't even go home after a nightgown because Lillian has given me two new ones. Allie can have her choice between the blue baby doll p.j.s or the pink one.

Allie and me carry food and plates back into the house. Dad cleans his new grill grate with a wire brush. Kate and Mom work at washing up the dishes. It is late and dark before we know it, and the cicadas sing their evening songs.

Allie and me wash up and slip on the starchy new p. j's. We pad through the dining room, calling our goodnights to the grown-ups sitting on the front porch. We stretch out sideways across the twin bed we will share and hang our hair down over our faces. From my wall, newspaper pictures of Colonel John Glenn and Valentina smile down at us.

I put on Allie's Brenda Lee record, and she sings a little bit, but I can tell her heart really isn't in it.

"What's the matter, Allie? Don't you like singing?"

"Singing's ok," Allie flops on her back and stretches one leg high up over her head. "I'm a ninth grader this year, and I guess maybe it's time I took a more responsible view of life," she says. "That's what Hank says."

"Hank, the award-winning stepdad? I can't believe you're listening to that maniac."

Allie hunches her shoulders, wiggles her foot like a dancer. "I've got a boyfriend, you know."

For a minute, I forget about my birthday. How could Allie get a boyfriend without telling me?

"No, you don't!"

"Un-huh,"

I sit up straight. Sometimes Allie tells whoppers. But it looks like she's serious.

"Who?"

"It's a secret," she says, pulling her leg forward, stretching.

A secret? From me?

"Well, do I at least *know* the boy?"

"He's not really a boy." Allie stretches out her other leg. "He's older. More manly."

Well, it's a lead pipe cinch it isn't Cal. Lindsey has him wound around her pinky finger tighter than a corkscrew. Sonny, Blinks, Kevin, or Eddie? They're all a year or two older than us.

It's not Eddie. Surely, it's not Eddie.

"You've met him occasionally."

"Occasionally?"

"We've kissed."

"Stop it, Allie!" I cover my ears.

"Twice!"

By now, I'm pacing the floor.

"Don't be so childish." She goes on. "Everyone does it."

"Not me!"

Suddenly, I wish my birthday could have happened two weeks ago. Now, it may be too late, even though Allie doesn't *look* different. I know she's changed.

I turn my back to Allie; stare out the darkened window. A face presses against my bedroom window screen. A face with a white mask.

Allie saw it, too.

We both scream. I jump back to bed with Allie.

Uncle Joe barrels in with Dad close at his heels.

"What is it?" Uncle Joe asks.

Allie and me clutch the sheets to our shoulders.

"A face at the window," I point one shaky finger.

Uncle Joe runs out of the room and races for the door. We hear him shouting for someone to "Stop!"

Dad snaps down the shade over the open window.

He growls. What do you expect if you loll around half-dressed with the shades up?" Instantly, I go from feeling frightened to dirty.

Dad runs his fingers through his crew-cut hair. He's angry and scared.

"You're growing up, Jessie. Men, well boys, they'll be interested and," Dad shakes his head. "You have to be more careful from here on. Understand?"

No.

No, I do not understand.

But I nod.

I picture my room, always with the shades pulled. I'll never be able to see the stars again or watch chickadees feed outside my window.

Dad turns and walks out of the room. He flicks off the light as he goes past the switch. "You girls go to sleep."

Allie and me crawl under the sheet and let our eyes adjust to the dark. We listen to the sounds of Uncle Joe and Dad coming back. The voices outside our window are hushed and difficult to make out.

"Call the police," Uncle Joe says.

Dad says, "No."

Uncle Joe mentions "crazy hero's heaven." And I wonder if the face at the window was Moon. It could have been. But

I don't know for sure. I wish whoever it was, their head would explode!

After a while, it is quiet again. The cicadas settle in, and the night goes back to its August stillness. My ancient swivel-fan clunks at each turn, hardly stirring the sticky air. I am trying not to think about boys and being careful. I try to concentrate on the good things about today—Eddie's necklace, Brett's magnifying glass, and Kate's Friendship 7 model.

Allie is crying.

"Allie," I whisper, "What's wrong?"

"It's my fault," Allie says between sniffs.

"What's your fault?" I put my hand on her bare arm. "The window-peeker? He's not your fault. And he's not my fault either."

I know this is true.

"No, the baby. It's my fault Mom lost the baby."

I can't say anything.

"Hank thinks it was a boy. Like Mom and him wanted. It's my fault the baby's gone."

"Allie, no, it's not. The baby, it probably wasn't right," Lillian's words come out of my mouth, and I want to strangle myself. "Sometimes things happen that way."

"No," Allie grabs my arm underneath the sheet. "I wished it away."

"What?"

"That night, we counted lightning bugs. I wished the baby dead."

"Oh, Allie, don't be a dope. You can't wish babies away. Besides, there were too many stars. It has to be the FIRST star."

"There were other times, too." Tears stream down Allie's pretty face. "I didn't want to be a big sister again. I didn't want the baby, and he died."

Allie cries harder.

I put my arms around her.

I remember wishing the window-peeker's head would explode. I think about the times Cal was angry. Maybe sometimes he wished I hadn't been born.

I think about wanting everything to be exactly as they were this evening. How could I have known I'd be wishing Allie misery for the rest of her life?

"I guess we better be careful what we wish for."

Allie cries a little longer. But I think she feels better.

I wish I did.

Is there a magic method for retracting wishes? I've never heard of one. I resort to the most mysterious authority I know.

"Dear God," I whisper. "Please help Allie feel better, and please, please don't explode the window-peeker's head. Thanks for listening, just me, Jessie."

CHAPTER 13

Odd Jobs

There's got to be a time limit on wishes. I'm hoping it's three days. Three's a good magical number. You get three wishes when a genie pops out of a lamp. Three little pigs can lick a big bad wolf. Three strikes, you're out. Yep, I definitely think after three days, my wish to blow up Mr. Moon's head should run out.

So, this is it. After today I'm in the clear. No more checking for exploding heads in the news. Good thing, too, because Cal got a real job at Gable's Grocery. Between the job and Lindsey, he's too busy for his home chores. So, guess who gets to take up the slack?

Now, along with hanging out laundry and dusting the living room, I get to mow grass and take out the garbage. Lucky me!

I hang the last set of socks, then slip over to my cherry tree. I pull myself up on the lowest limb for a rest. I can see Moon from here. He's mangling Mrs. Moon's zinnia patch with a hoe. I really was worried he might be the window-peeker. What if, after surviving a war, Moon's head blew open? There's probably a special prison for people who wish evil on crazy war heroes. Of course, prison might be preferable to what's coming—school starts tomorrow.

In our end of Stevenston, junior and senior highs share the same building. The junior high classes are on the second level, and the senior high meets on the first. But you've got to go in on the first level to get to the second, which means we'll be mingling with the high school kids every day before and after school. I'm not too anxious to meet up with Brody Beaman in the halls. He hasn't come around since that day at the state fair. I figure he's plotting his revenge, and I'll be likely to catch it at school.

At least I'll have Allie to show me the ropes. This is her third year at good old Stevenson Junior/Senior High; we won't have any classes together unless I join the all-school choir. I'm wondering how well I have to sing to make it. I'm guessing it'd be better than a tree frog croaking. I was trying out a little Sugar Shack when Mom called to me from the back door.

She walks toward me and my tree. Her face is flushed from the heat of the kitchen. Dad is due home this evening, so even though it's about a hundred and ten in the shade today, Mom is baking him a red velvet cake.

"I need you to come in and watch the cake for me." Mom pushes back a damp tendril of hair from her forehead. "Mrs. Moon phoned asking for Cal. This is his day to bring her groceries. Of course, he can't leave his work. I guess I'll have to run over for them myself."

"I'll do it." It was out of my mouth before my brain kicked in

Mom lifts her face to a tender breeze. "The cake has about fifteen minutes left to bake. Mind you, don't tromp around, and don't go banging the oven door…"

"No, I mean, I'll go to the grocery for Mrs. Moon," I say, imagining the dollar tip Cal gets for doing this errand. I picture it folded neatly and tucked inside my shorts pocket. There's also the air-conditioning unit Mr. Gable installed in his store this June…

"I don't think that's a good idea, Jessie."

"Mom, I'll be *fine*! I'm doing all Cal's other chores. Besides, even if Moon was the window-peeker, he's busy now."

I point across our backyards. Moon has moved on from the zinnias to Mrs. Moon's vegetable patch. Cabbage leaves float around his calves like miniature satellites.

Mom sighs. "Poor Mrs. Moon. All right, I suppose you can do it *once*. After this, she can find someone else."

Okay,' I jump down and dust off the seat of my shorts

"I'll keep an eye on Moon." Mom whispers. She starts toward the back fence. I try hard to keep pace with her.

Mom sets a hand on my right shoulder. "Scoot over there around to the front. And don't spend a minute more than necessary."

I scoot as fast as my shorter leg allows.

I'm around the west side when I hear, "Hello, Mr. Moon. Are you gardening today?"

I slip around the corner onto the front porch. I step up one clump, two, and ring the bell.

Mrs. Moon opens the door. Mrs. Moon smiles. "Hello, Jessica Louise." She's a thin-faced woman with kinky white hair. Her eyes are a shade of blue that reminds me of jeans about a zillion years old. Her house dress has an apron tied around her waist. The apron says: "Kissin' don't last, but cookin' do."

"I thought your mother was coming."

"She's got a velvet cake in the oven."

"I see," says Mrs. Moon. Her eyebrows squinch together. "Please, come in for a minute. Lenny's busy outside." She swings the screen door further out and presses herself against the doorframe to let me pass.

"I do love a bit of girl talk now and then."

The Moon's living room is tiny. A green and red linoleum floor torn around the edges and worn through in spots. They have an old-fashioned radio standing on the floor, a television, a ratty-looking sofa, and there's an overstuffed chair and a bookcase.

"Make yourself at home, Jessie," Mrs. Moon says. "I'll finish writing my list." She leaves me standing alone in the living room.

My stomach feels like I'm on an elevator dropping too fast. Moon will be happy destroying their gardens and how long Mom can keep him distracted after that. Suddenly this job doesn't seem like such a great idea.

I'm too nervous to sit, so I wander around the tiny room. I pick up an ashtray made of plaster and seashells from the top of the TV. There's an outline of buttocks and bare feet on it and the legend. "I made an impression in Florida."

"I appreciate you doing this," Mrs. Moon calls from the kitchen.

"That's okay," I call back and move on to the shoulder-high bookcase.

In the bookcase, there are mostly frayed volumes of Western stories. On top of the bookcase are three framed pictures. First, President Kennedy gives us his profile: chin-lifted, handsome features. I would like to have a picture of Mr. Kennedy, but my dad doesn't like the President. He'd never allow such a thing.

"I hope I'm not ordering too much for you to carry," Mrs. Moon calls again. "But I have special bags with handles to use. You look like a strong girl."

"I am strong," I flex my muscles.

Mrs. Moon smiles. "So, I see."

I put down President Kennedy and pick up the next picture. This one's a smiling young couple dressed in old-fashioned clothes. The girl is holding a bunch of daisies and wearing a long filmy dress. The boy is in an army uniform with close-fitting leggings and a round sort of hat. He's grinning like he's just been handed a zillion dollars.

I slant the picture toward the window. The girl is pretty. About the same age as Lindsey. The army guy is probably only a little older than she. Then it hits me. This is Mr. and Mrs. Moon!

Somehow, in spite of all the stories of Moon's heroism in WWI, I'd never once imagined him young, handsome, and full of hope.

Mrs. Moon comes out of the kitchen. She has a sheet of lined paper in one hand and a pair of canvas shopping bags in the other. She stops in the living room archway. "I see you've found Lenny and me. Didn't he cut a fine figure in his uniform?"

"Yes, Ma'am."

Mrs. Moon crosses the room. She gives me her bags and her list. I hand her the picture. She traces Mr. Moon's portrait with her finger.

"He was a medic in the Great War, you know. That's what they called it, World War I. It was supposed to be the last war we'd ever have to fight." She looks off into the distance. Remembering. "He never carried a gun. He helped the wounded. He won a medal for heroism. Did you know that?"

"My grandpa said Mr. Moon is a hero. He says Mr. Moon got knocked out by a cannonball that exploded near him."

"Well, your grandpa is right. But there's more to Lenny's hurt than that. There were so many wounded." Mrs. Moon sighs. "He saw so much blood, so much death all around him…" Mrs. Moon sets her wedding picture back on the shelf. "Lenny's mind got all mixed up. Maybe that's a blessing. Maybe not remembering…." Mrs. Moon says. "Still, there are some times he knows what's happening."

"I'm sorry."

Mrs. Moon waves it away. "I didn't mean to go into all that." She hands me the third picture. "This is our daughter, Ellen."

Ellen is a thin girl with light eyes. Her hands are tented beneath her chin in a glamorous way.

"Ellen lives in California."

"Oh?" I stare down at the picture.

"I expect you've never seen her," she said. "She married young."

I hand the picture back.

"Her husband has a wonderful job in the film industry." Mrs. Moon replaces the picture. "Ellen acts in movies, too."

"Truly?" I think Allie's going to be delirious.

"Yes, truly." Did you ever see the one at the Empress?"

"The one with all the chariot races and big horses?"

Mrs. Moon nods.

"Yeah, Dad took us to see it."

"Then you've seen our Ellen," Mrs. Moon smiles. "She was in two of the crowd scenes. The director was very pleased with her."

"Sincerely?"

"Absolutely," Mrs. Moon straightened her apron.

"Who would have guessed it? A movie star from our very own neighborhood?"

"Exactly!" Says Mrs. Moon. "Ellen's going to send for Lenny and me as soon as she's established. Yes, indeed, we'll wing our way out to sunny California to live with our Ellen."

"Wow!"

I look around the living room, and my heart sinks. I remember hospital parents promising their children ponies and trips to amusement parks. That's great, except I figured out some of us were in worse trouble than a gimpy right leg foot. Some of us wouldn't be going home, let alone ride the rides. If Ellen Moon hadn't returned for her parents in that much time, then maybe parents aren't the only ones who make promises they can't keep.

Moon's back door opens and slams shut. I step toward the front door with Mrs. Moon's list and shopping bags.

She follows and puts a hand on my arm. "Jessie, about the other night…"

I freeze in the doorway; my heart thumps. Moon is shuffling through their kitchen, but Mrs. Moon seems intent on having her say.

"It wasn't Lenny at your window," Mrs. Moon says. "He was home in bed."

I nod.

"You don't need to be afraid of Lenny, really. He's a gentle soul."

I look into Mrs. Moon's faded eyes. I see she believes what she's saying. She may only be pretending about the California thing, but she believes Moon is gentle. I see she will still believe this even after she finds her zinnias and cabbages chopped to pieces.

Like the hospital kids and parents, I think maybe Mrs. Moon *needs* to believe it.

"Yes, Ma'am."

Mrs. Moon lets go of my arm, and I step out onto the porch. "I'll have some lemonade waiting for you when you return." She promises.

"That'll be good." I hurry on down the walk.

"Jessie!" She calls. I turn at the end. "Um, be sure you check the eggs for cracks."

"I will," I promise.

CHAPTER 14

Eggs

I stay in Gable's Grocery as long as I can. The air inside is so cool it's a wonder anyone ever leaves. Gables are proud of their new air conditioning unit. They have red and blue streamers tied to the vents, so people won't miss seeing it.

Mrs. Gable totals up the bill and charges it to the Moons' account.

"Did you check the eggs for cracks, Sweetie?" Mrs. Gable asks. "The Moons are particular about their eggs."

"Yes, Ma'am."

Cal stands at the end of the counter wearing a long white apron over his jeans and t-shirt. I bite my cheek to keep from laughing. He looks comical to me, masquerading as a grownup person.

He stows my groceries in Mrs. Moon's bags and then pushes the door open for me. "Thanks for shopping at Gable's," he says.

Like I wasn't his little sister but some ordinary customer.

I bump out onto the sidewalk, where the heat blasts away. Sweat pops out all over me again. I wish I'd forgotten something on Mrs. Moon's list so I could go back inside.

At least there'll be lemonade waiting for me, I think, and begin my three blocks walk back. About halfway down the second block, I hear.

"Hey, crip!"

I freeze in my tracks. I haven't seen Brody since the fair. Truth is, I was hoping *never* to see him again. I hear his heavy footfalls from behind me. There's no sense thinking I can run. Even without the Moons' groceries weighing me down, I could never beat Brody in a foot race.

He draws even with me and nudges me with his shoulder. It could be a friendly nudge. But probably isn't.

"Tripped anymore unsuspecting people?" His voice sounds odd, and I turn to look at him. His forehead is scabbed over mostly, but there's a large swatch of white gauze stretched across his nose and fastened to his cheekbones by massive amounts of white tape.

Like a mask.

"It was you!" I say out loud.

"What?" Brody says. "Like you don't recognize the guy you tripped?"

"No!" I'm sure now. "It was you at my window…."

"You're crazy," Brody sneers. "I wasn't within a mile of your stupid birthday party. I don't go where I ain't invited."

"Then how'd you know I was talking about my party?"

"You crazy? Everybody heard about the famous winda peeker." Brody says. "An' everybody with a lick of brain in their head figures it was Moon."

I shake my head. "I *saw* you! Your bandages were a mask."

Brody grabs my arm hard. "Listen, you don't go spreadin' lies about me, hear?" Brody tightens his grip.

I think my arm might pop.

"I got plans. Real plans, not rocket ship to the moon pipe dreams like some people. You ain't allowed to mess 'em up with your lies."

My legs tremble. My stomach turns over, imagining Brody Beaman staring in at me in my baby doll p.j.s.

"You better keep your lip zipped!" He gives my arm another painful shake. The groceries spill from Mrs. Moon's bags. "You hear me, Crip?"

"Get away from me!" I yell and somehow wrench my arm out of his grip. I gather up the spilled groceries: Bread and flow-through teabags, pickles, tomato juice, back into Mrs. Moon's bags. But I am not fast enough to save the eggs. Brody tramps down hard on the cardboard carton, and yellow yokes spurt all over the steaming sidewalk.

Oh, God! Oh, God! The Moons' eggs. What will I do about the eggs?

Brody hooks a booted shoe under the caved-in carton and gives it a punt. It lands in scruffy grass and rolls down an incline. He points an index finger at me like a gun.

"Remember to keep your lips zipped, Crip." Brody Beaman says and saunters away.

It takes time to get my legs and hands working together. I put everything into Mrs. Moon's bags. Suddenly, I'm giggling. *Brody made a rhyme. This crip will keep her lip zipped.* I tell myself to stop giggling. But it's uphill work.

I turn back to Gables' Grocery. Mrs. Gable knows Chrismans always pay our bills. Surely, she will trust me for a new fifty-cent carton of eggs.

In some crazy way, I figure maybe this is a kind of justice. After accusing a war hero like Mr. Moon of window-peeping, I think I owe him more than uncracked eggs.

CHAPTER 15

First Day

Ihave my book fees in an envelope, my hair up in a ponytail, and my best corrective oxfords spit-shined. I have a new skirt and blouse from the J.C. Penney catalog. Cal gave me a wolf whistle at breakfast. That felt fine.

But if I didn't have Allie walking with me up the mile-long concrete sidewalk to Stevenston Junior/Senior High, I'd be a general wreck.

A flagpole sits at the end of the walk. There's the Stars and Stripes on the pole, of course, and flying below that is the Illinois flag and below that, the blue and orange of the Stevenson Wildcats.

I step down once, twice as the walk enters a dip in the school's huge lawn. I feel homesick for the cozy playground of elementary school. I miss the swings, the jungle gym, and the chalked outlines for hopscotch.

"What if I get lost?"

"You won't get lost," Allie smiles. "All your classes are on the second floor, except for the gym and cafeteria. They're downstairs. Here's the most important thing. Do *NOT* step on the wildcat square in the middle of the lobby floor. Jocks and cheerleaders and student council dweebs spaz if you step on the cat."

"Okay."

"You'll see the tables to register when we first get in. Junior high on the south wall, Senior high on the north. There will be signs on the walls above the tables. Everything goes alphabetically by last name. We'll get registered then we will meet at the bottom of the central stairs. I'll help you find your homeroom."

"Good," I say. "Which way is south, again?"

"Towards Gables Grocery."

"Right."

"No, left!" Allie and me laugh at that.

This is my first time registering for school without Mom. Mom thought Cal would help me, but he's too busy mooning around Lindsey to bother. That's ok. I'd rather have Allie with me any day.

A couple of senior high girls go around us, sniffing as if we smell bad. We ignore them.

"There won't be much work today. The teachers hand out textbooks, and you'll get your locker assignment. Memorize your locker combination as quickly as you can. There are thieves in this school."

"Okay," I say. "What do I do when I throw up?"

"Say excuse my urp!"

We are standing at a triple set of doors leading into the building. Every time a door swings open, a roaring jumble of voices leaks outside.

"Ready?" Allie asks.

"No!"

"Good. Me neither." Allie is as nervous as I am.

She pushes open one of the doors, and we walk into pandemonium together.

I get in line at the A-D table. I've creased the envelope with Mom's check in it so many times it looks like an accordion. I try to straighten it out and look for familiar faces at the same time. Blinks Malloy and Sonny Kramer are two tables down from me. I shout, "Hey, guys!" But they don't hear me over the hundreds of voices in the room.

I look around for Lindsey and Cal. I find them tucked under the central set of stairs. Lindsey leans against the wall, and Cal stands in front of her. One hand is pressed against the wall above her shoulder. The other is on her waist. They aren't necking in front of God and everybody, but they're next to it.

I look for Allie and spot her in the next line over. She's not towards the end, though, like I am, but in front of Kevin Fombelle, who is only two people back from the table. He must have given her up. Allie smiles at him and bats her eyes at Kevin, and I wonder if he is her secret boyfriend. My heart lifts a little at the thought.

Lines move quickly. The teachers have registration down to an art. I gawk around, looking for other people I know, trying to slow my erratic heartbeat. I see guys in letterman sweaters (even though it's eighty-five degrees in the shade today) and girls whose skirts are pushing the school's limit on length.

A gray-haired lady walks around with a yardstick, tapping girls' shoulders, demonstrating how far above the knee Stevenston Junior/Senior High will allow their skirts to be. I don't have any worries that way. Dad would freak big time if my knees showed. Besides, I'm not anxious to show off the scabs left over from sliding into home base last week.

"It's your turn." The boy behind me nudges. I step up to the registration table.

"Name?" asks the wiry man seated there. His name tag reads, "Mr. Tanner, Mathematics."

"Jessie Chrisman," I croak.

He runs a pencil down a page of names. "Jessica Louise Chrisman?"

"Yes, sir."

He makes a check mark beside my name. "Do you have your book rental fee?"

I hand him my crinkled envelope. He tears off one end and shakes out the check. He writes "pd" by my name, fills out a receipt, and hands it to me.

" Miss. Martin," he says to the square-shouldered woman next to him. "Do you have a schedule for Miss. Chrisman?"

"I do, Mr. Tanner" Miss. Martin hands me a thin rectangle of paper with my name typed across the top. "It looks as if I'll be seeing you for science, Miss. Chrisman. I'll warn you, everyone in my class is required to enter a project in the January Science Fair." Miss. Martin smiles at me. "So, you can be thinking about what you'd most like to do."

"Yes, Ma'am."

I glance down at the paper disguised as my schedule. I can't make heads or tails of its code. There's a set of columns—titled Hr., Sub., Rm., Sec., Inst, Cr.

I need Allie.

I head off in the direction I last saw her, scanning the crowd for a glimpse of her. I spot her at the bottom of the stairs. I excuse myself through a forest of elbows and knees. At last, I make it to a clear spot in the center of the floor. I raise my arm to wave. I hear, "Hey, Crip!" from behind me, and I freeze.

"Didn't no one never tell you not to walk on the Wildcat?" Brody Beaman steps in front of me and gives me a shove. His forehead is mostly healed, but his nose looks as if it's taken a permanent detour to the left.

I swallow hard and tighten my stomach in case he's going to punch me right here in front of Miss. Martin and everybody.

He points at my feet. I look down and see I'm standing smack between the wildcat's staring green eyes. "Better move, Jessie, before some football hero throws a flyin' tackle on you."

"Oh!" I cry and jump off to the side. Back to the safety of the plain gray flecked tile of the regular floor. "Thanks," I say. I'm having some real eye trouble because it looks like Brody's smiling at me. It's disorienting.

"S'okay," he says. "They oughta put up one them rope gates like they've got in the movie houses around this here cat. That'd keep people off it."

"Yeah?"

"Maybe I'll send 'em back some money so they can buy one," Brody says. "Yeah, and I'll spring for a plaque, too. It'll read rope gate courtesy of Brody. Beaman, USMC.

I blink, thinking I've crossed over into another dimension at some point. Maybe on some planet where everyone speaks in an alphabetic code but me.

"Well, I better go," Brody says, turning back toward the entrance doors.

I realize he's leaving.

"Wait!" I'm really feeling strange. The real me would never call for Brody to come back. "Aren't you staying for school?"

"Naw, I'm gettin' outta this dump." He turns back. "I only come in to show 'em my papers. My old man don't want no truant officers beaten' down his door."

"Papers?"

"Enlistment papers. You're looking at a United States Marine," he says. "Leastwise, I will be once I get through with my basic training."

"When do you leave?"

"Tomorrow," Brody smiles again. This time the smile only lifts one side of his mouth. He moves his fingers across his lips in a zipping motion.

I swallow hard. "Well," I say. "Good luck."

"Same back at'cha," he says then. "Hey, Jessie. Maybe I'll write you."

I can't think of one reason why Brody Beaman would *want* to write me.

"Yeah, you could tell all the other little seventh graders you gotta friend in the Marines. It'd give you a rep."

I stare at him, trying to imagine Brody as my pen pal, or anyone's pen pal, for that matter.

"It'd keep the lowlifes from messing with you." Brody goes on. "Tell 'em they bother you; your friend the marine will beat the crap outta 'em when he gets home."

Once Brody leaves, I figure the lowlife population in Stevenston will be pretty much depleted.

"Just an idea." He shrugs and pulls the door open.

I feel the crush of students behind me. Maybe I'm wrong in regards to Stevenston's supply of lowlifes.

"Okay," I call after him.

"Yeah?"

"Yeah," I say. "Write to me, and I'll write back."

Brody tips me a wink. "Good deal," he says. "Tell the rest of our bunch I said, Bye, will ya?"

Our bunch?

"Sure," I say.

Brody Beaman walks out the triple doors of Stevenston Jr/Sr High into the bright September sunshine.

CHAPTER 16

B'lunch

I look down at my schedule again. The same unreadable code still marches across the top.

I need Allie.

Allie helps me figure out the code on my schedule and find my locker. Then we go our separate ways until lunch. I make it through English and social studies in the first two hours and then onto science in the third.

I know this will be my favorite class. We meet in a room with high shiny black tables and four-legged stools instead of chairs. Miss. Martin passes out our textbooks and talks to us about the January Science Fair. Excitement shines from her eyes.

"Everyone is expected to present an entry," she says. "It can be anything that interests you, but your project will need to be approved by me. So, be thinking of what you might like to do. I want a written proposal describing your project by the middle of next month."

I don't have to think for long. I know exactly what I want to do. I'm almost finished building my birthday model of Friendship 7, John Glenn's space module. I'll bet lots of kids will be doing that.

But what will make my project special is I'm going to build the Russian spaceship as well: The Vostok 6. That's the one Valentina Tereshkova orbited the Earth in. I wish I had better pictures of both Glenn and Tereshkova. The newspaper shots I have taped to my walls are beginning to turn yellow. I wonder where I could get new ones.

I spend the rest of science class planning the materials I'll need for the Vostok and wondering if Eddie will help me.

After science, I find my way downstairs to the lunchroom. That's easy. I could lift up my feet and be carried along on a wave of hungry students.

Allie waits for me by the lunchroom door. She reaches out a hand and pulls me to her.

"How'd you do?" she asks.

"Okay, I think."

"Good!" We join the mob of students standing in line for their lunches. Teachers come into the lunchroom, too, but they don't have to wait in line. They make their selections and huddle together in a tight group at the first tables out from the food line.

"Steer clear of the chili," Allie says, "or else you'll toot all afternoon. But the potato soup is good."

We load up our trays and find seats in a sort of middle ground between the junior and senior high sections of the lunchroom. Kevin, Sonny, and Blinks join us. Eddie slides his lunch tray next to mine. Except for Lindsey and Cal, our whole neighborhood is eating together. The noise in the lunchroom is astronomical.

Eddie pulls out his schedule and jabs an elbow in my ribs to let me know he wants to see mine.

I unfold it from my skirt pocket and pass it to him. He points to my science teacher, Miss. Martin's name, and leans close to me. His lips nearly touch my right ear. His breath is warm. He asks his one-word question. Which, for a miracle, I understand.

"Project?"

I nod, and he turns his head to give me his ear. "Friendship 7," I whisper back.

Eddie gives me the thumb and index finger signal for perfect.

I lean in close again. "*And* Vostok 6!"

Eddie slaps his forehead. He leans in again and whispers. "Excellent!" Then points to himself. "Want help?"

Maybe he is a mind reader. "Absolutely!"

Eddie grins and unwraps his turkey sandwich.

"Man!" Kevin shouts above the din of students. "I hope we don't ever have a fire during "B" lunch. We'd never hear the alarm."

"Yeah," Sonny hollers. "We'd be trash. They'd have to call old man Beaman to come and haul us away."

That reminds me of Brody joining the Marines. I shout the story of his enlistment to my friends.

"Well!" Kevin says when I finish. "It'll be a dull year without Brody punching somebody's lights out on a regular basis."

"Yeah," says Blinks. "We're gonna Miss the old jarhead. About like we miss pimples on our noses."

Allie keeps her head down, stirring her potato soup until there's no heat left in it. She doesn't say a word.

The end of the "B" lunch bell must have rung somewhere because people are picking up their trays and moving out of the lunchroom. Allie and me and the guys do the same.

I am the last of our group to deposit my empty lunch tray on the cafeteria counter. I look at my friends standing together, waiting to walk Sonny and me to the central stairs. I have to smile.

"Our bunch." I think.

CHAPTER 17

Letters Home

"I'm home, Mom!" I yell. The front screen door slams behind me.

The October sun slants golden across our living room floor. I go into the dining room and set down a paper grocery sack full of kite sticks and tissue paper on the dining room table. Eddie and me have scavenged these building materials from his house for my model of Vostok 6.

I wanted to use tin cans, but shaping the sharp edges into the sphere-shaped module was too hard on the fingers. So, we're going to try this method instead. Eddie thinks we can paint it up to look like metal. Man! If the spaceship designers have as much trouble as we do building their rockets, it's a wonder anybody ever gets into orbit.

The whole house smells of freshly baked bread, and my mouth waters. Mom must be on her second batch because there's a loaf already sliced and waiting for me, along with a jar of cinnamon apple butter. I grab up a heel, slather some of the apple butter across it, and take a big bite. Then I go in search of some milk.

"There's a letter for you on the table, Jessie," Mom calls. "And Mrs. Moon asked if you could come over as soon as you can."

"Okay," I say around my mouthful. I finish my snack and pick up the letter. It's addressed to Miss. J. Chrisman and it bears the return address of Brody Beaman, USMC, Parris Island, South Carolina.

Well, I'll be dipped in spit! Brody wrote. The envelope is thick like it has several pages tucked inside. Who knew Brody could spell so many words? I stick the letter in my skirt pocket and run over to Mrs. Moon's.

I've been bringing the Moons their groceries ever since that first time. Sometimes I help Mrs. Moon with the cleaning. She always pays me something. I'm getting used to Moon's yelling. It hardly even bothers me anymore.

Moon opens the door before I ring the bell. "Over the top!" he yells, waving a scrawny arm in front of my face. "Where's your gas mask, soldier?"

"I left it in the trenches."

"That won't do, soldier," Moon scolds. "How do you expect to survive the gas?"

"Lenny, dear," Mrs. Moon appears from the back room. "Let Jessie in, she's come to help."

Moon whirls on his heel to scowl at Mrs. Moon, and me. I duck around him.

"Darned irregular," he complains. "Sending them younger and younger these days." He shuffles into their living room and plops down on the couch, muttering.

"I need you to help me clear out the spare bedroom, Jessie," she says. "Our girl is coming home for a visit. Just look at this letter that came today."

Mrs. Moon holds out a sheet of pale blue stationery. The words are written in gold ink in a fancy looping hand.

September 30th, 1963

Dear Mother,

I am delighted to tell you I will be coming to Chicago later this month. I have an inside track for a prime role in their live on-stage production. At any rate, as I am presently between engagements, I thought I would come along early to visit you and reconnect with my Midwestern roots before the auditions.

I shall travel by train. Can you arrange for someone to pick me up on Saturday, October 26? I will arrive at 3:45 p.m.

Please let me know as soon as possible.

Love, Ellen.

"I wish our mail service was a little faster. I've already lost a week of preparing. Isn't it exciting? Our little girl is coming home! Now we'll need to take the curtains down in her room—oh, I wish I could buy new ones. And the bedspread needs washed as well. The floor needs waxed and the windows cleaned. Can you help me with all that?"

"Sure!" Seeing Mrs. Moon excited gets me worked up, too. I'm thinking how thrilled Allie will be to have a genuine star of stage and screen coming right here to our very own neighborhood. Maybe Ellen Moon can give Allie a few pointers on how to get started in show business.

At the very least, we might both get autographed pictures out of the deal. Allie's crazy about autographed pictures. She's got one of every one of her favorite singers taped on the ceiling over her bed. She sent off for a piano player, too, but that one hasn't arrived.

I hand the letter back to Mrs. Moon, and she tucks it in her apron pocket. "Let's get started." She gives me a laundry basket, and I follow her into their spare bedroom. "It's been ages since these have been washed. I hope they don't fall apart in the machine."

She moves a short bench from the dressing table to the bedroom window. "Can you climb, Jessie?"

"Like a monkey," I say.

"Good!" Mrs. Moon holds out her hand to help me, and I step up onto the bench, good foot first, and begin taking curtains from their rods. She whips the spread from off the bed and deposits it in the basket.

"My washing machine is too small to accommodate the spread. Can you carry these to the Laundromat and do them up?"

I finish with the second set of curtains and lay them on top of the spread. "Sure, but I'll need to stop in and tell Mom where I'm going."

"Yes, of course," Mrs. Moon says. She digs into her "cookin' and kissin'" apron pocket and brings up a fistful of change. She counts out enough for the washer and dryer and enough for one of the little boxes of laundry soap from the vending machines. Then she adds two more dimes.

"You'll need a soda while you're waiting and maybe a candy bar as well to keep up your strength."

I put Mrs. Moon's change in the pocket of my skirt and cradle the laundry basket on my hip. I follow Mrs. Moon out of the bedroom and into the living room, where Mr. Moon is sprawled across their sofa, snoring like a rhinoceros.

"He's always like this after his treatment, poor dear." Mrs. Moon says, gazing at her husband. "And they've switched his medicine again. It really knocks him out of it."

Out of it is exactly where Moon belongs, I think. But I nod my head in sympathy.

"I'll wash the windows while you're doing these up."

I never saw anyone happier than Mrs. Moon about a load of work visited upon her. Still, a movie actress is coming to Stevenston, and I can't help but be a little hyped up myself.

The Laundromat smells equal parts of sweat socks, peed diapers, and bleach. Machines spin and whirl, and water swishes inside the glass-fronted machines like miniature sudsy oceans.

There's hardly anyone here at this time of day, and I have my pick of the large machines. I peer inside one to be certain it's clean, then load Mrs. Moon's spread and curtains in, slam the door, and test it to be sure it closed good.

Once, I came here to help Allie do her mom's wash, and we didn't get the doors closed all the way. Diapers, dresses, towels, and Hank's boxer shorts streamed out the door in foamy waves of soapy water. We almost got banned from the laundromat!

This time I'm extra careful. I put in the miniature box of soap powder, drop in her change and turn the knob to get the whole thing started. I watch for a minute to be certain it's all working, then I saunter on over to the vending machines. I drop in my dimes and get out a paper cup of soda from one machine and a peanut candy bar from another. I sit at one of the square tables in front of the laundromat's picture window and take a sip from my soda pop.

Now, I have time to read Brody's letter. When I rip open the envelope, I get a real surprise. There's another envelope sealed and folded inside. Paper clipped to that is a little square of paper. The words scrawled across it make me gasp.

Jessie,

Give this letter to Allie and don't tell no one about it!

Brody Beaman, USMC

P.S. I'm learning how to shoot really good.

CHAPTER 18

Secret Agent

The whole of "B" lunch, while everyone else talks about Ellen Moon's trip to Stevenston, Brody's letter burns a hole in my skirt pocket. Eddie is drawing his idea on a napkin about balloons and string and paste as an alternate method for making Vostok, but I can't keep my mind on it. He taps two fingers on my forehead. But I shake my head.

"Can't think right now, sorry."

Eddie shrugs.

My gut burns with worry. What if I don't give Allie Brody's letter? I could tear it into tiny pieces and flush them down the toilet. She'd think Brody never wrote to her. Letters get lost in the mail all the time. Look how long it took Ellen Moon's to get from California to Stevenston.

Who would know? Well, Mom would know, but no one else. That'd be safe. Wouldn't it?

Then there's the problem of when Brody comes home, which he's bound to do. I mean, basic training can't go on forever, can it? Then what do I say when he wants to know what happened to Allie's letter? Besides, I keep remembering his P.S.

So, finally, when we're filing out from lunch, I grab Allie's arm, and we drop back from Kevin and the others. I slide the letter out of my pocket and hiss, "Special delivery."

Allie glances at the envelope, and her face flushes. She grabs it out of my hand and slides it inside her geography book.

"Thanks," she whispers.

"You're not welcome!" I snap. "Why didn't you *tell* me?"

"I couldn't!"

"Right! I thought we were best friends."

"We are!"

"Yeah, well, you're not acting like it."

"Look, Jessie, I promised Brody we'd keep our love a secret."

"Love? Oh, please, I'm going to throw up!" I turn to walk away, but she grabs my arm.

"He says people will try to break us up. That they wouldn't approve."

"He's got that right! Allie, what are you thinking? He's too *old* for you."

Allie stiffens. "What about Cal and Lindsey? Isn't *she* too old for him?"

"That's different."

"How is it different?" Allie demands. "Will you just tell me that, Jessie Chrisman?"

"I'd be happy to, Allie Hart," I say. "That's different because Lindsey Smith isn't mean as a snake, and Brody Beaman is!"

"You don't know the real Brody," Allie says.

"I know him as well as I want to," I say. "He threatened to shoot me in *my* little love note."

Allie pales. "He never!"

I shove the little square of paper Brody paper clipped to Allie's letter under her nose.

"That doesn't mean a thing. He's just proud of what he's learning. Why do you always put the worst meaning on anything he says?"

I stare at Allie, wondering if an alien has taken over my best friend's body and she's somewhere trapped inside, screaming to get out.

"I'm going to be late for math," I pull away from her and hurry down the hall.

Allie runs after me.

"Wait! Jessie!"

But I don't stop.

She trots up beside me. "I need you to send my letters back to him."

"No!"

"Please, Jessie, you're the only one I can trust."

I keep walking.

"I'd do it for you," Allie says.

That stops me. "I'd never *ask* you to."

"I know. But *I am* asking you."

"Aaugh! All right, I'll do it!" I give in. "But just once, so you can tell him I gave you his crummy letter."

The bell rings, signaling the beginning of the fourth hour

Allie hugs me. "You won't be sorry, Jessie."

"I already am," I say and race up the stairs to Mr. Tanner's math.

CHAPTER 19

Friendship 7

It's a fine October Saturday morning, and the Friendship 7 model is finished and sitting on a specially-made stand on Dad's basement workbench. It's waiting for me to write a report giving every detail I know about John Glenn's space module.

I know a lot. For instance, the 7 in Friendship 7 stands for the number of men chosen to be the first United States Astronauts. The Friendship part of my science project is not a problem. However, the Vostok 6 is another matter.

With the cold war on between Russia and the U.S., the hobby shops around town aren't exactly falling over themselves to stock model plans for the Russian spacecraft. So, Eddie and me are making up our own. At least we're trying to.

We have already tested some methods for modeling Valentina's Vostok 6 (which a person would think would be easy as pie since it looks like nothing so much as a round metal ball), but it's proving to be harder than we thought.

We tried tin cans. They were too sharp to handle once they were cut. Then we tried kite sticks soaked in water, bent into spheres, and covered with paper-mâché, which looked pretty good. Except every time I picked up the model, my finger went through the Vostok's skin.

Now we're covering blown-up balloons with paste-dipped strings. We're doing two at a time in case we have a system failure in one, we'll have a backup Vostok. Eddie has a blue balloon in the first string-wrap stage, and my red one is on a second layer.

Dad's ancient radio is tuned to the only station it can get in the basement, KSTV, which plays a mongrel mix of show tunes and country, but that's better than no music, I guess.

"You're sure once the string dries, it won't matter if the balloon bursts?" I ask Eddie for about the zillionth time.

"Shouldn't," Eddie says.

"That's good because I'm tired of trying to think up new ways to make the Vostok."

Eddie punches my arm playfully. "Impatient one," he says.

I run my fingers through my hair to make it stand on end. "Who vishes to consult vitt Madam Magda?"

Eddie flips a gob of paste at me. I dodge it easily.

Ever since our visit to Madam Magda, I've been able to understand Eddie's speech. At first, it was only when he whispered, and that's still how I hear him best. But now, even when he speaks normally, I can make out what he's saying. I've pretty much replaced Cal as Eddie's interpreter for our friends.

An announcer comes on extolling the virtues of men's hair treatment. I dip another string in my bowl of paste and layer it on my balloon.

"Eddie?"

"Hm?"

"I've been wondering about something."

He cocks an eyebrow and waits for me to explain.

"Does everyone understand you when you whisper?"

Eddie shrugs.

"What do you mean you don't know?"

He crooks a paste-covered finger at me. I lean toward him, and he puts his lips next to my ear. "I only whisper to you."

I blush, beginning down in my toes and finishes at the tips of my ears. I duck my head and dip another string in the paste.

The announcer plays a sappy love song, and I think my string will melt right out from under my fingers. It feels like the longest song in history. It stops just as Mom calls to us from the top of the stairs, "Time for a break."

She balances a tray of apple cider and warm brownies down the stairs.

"I'm sorry I don't have the astronauts' favorite snack, freeze-dried mush in a tube," Mom teases.

Eddie snaps his fingers, meaning "Dog-gone!"

Mom slides the tray on the workbench between us. She claims one of the workbench stools. Eddie and me help ourselves to the goodies.

"Building the Vostok must be hungry work," Mom says.

We agree between bites.

"The mail came early today," Mom remarks a little too casually.

She pulls an airmail envelope from the pocket of her slacks. "You got another letter from Brody, Jessie. It's a thick one again." She turns the envelope around in her hands. "That boy's going to break himself up buying postage."

I swallow hard and reach for my cider.

Mom lays the envelope on the tray.

Eddie stops in mid-reach for a second brownie.

I let the envelope lay where she pushed it.

"He must be learning a lot of new things in the Marines," Mom says. "I'd enjoy hearing about Brody. Wouldn't you, Eddie?"

Eddie nods hard.

I know Mom's worried about Brody's letters, and this is her not-so-subtle version of psychology. Between parental privilege and peer pressure, she figures I'll tell her what she wants to know.

"So?" Mom prompts.

The letter sits on the tray like a cobra getting ready to strike. If I open the envelope, Allie's secret will be out, which would be a relief. But I don't think I can betray her trust and keep her friendship. If there's one thing I know that's almost impossible to repair, it's broken trust. But Mom is waiting for an answer, and so is Eddie. I have to say something. So, I settle for some of the truth.

"He's learning to shoot a rifle."

"And?" Mom says.

"That's pretty much it." I pick up Brody's letter and slide it into my jeans pocket.

"I guess people have a right to their privacy," Mom says. "If you're all finished with these things, I'll clear them away."

Mom picks up the snack tray and starts back upstairs.

Eddie's giving me a look I can't return.

The radio announces the next song. It's about this singer who needs to choose which is the right thing to do.

I know just how that singer feels.

CHAPTER 20

Stage And Screen

I feel like a courier pigeon, shuttling letters between Allie and Brody almost every week. I hide the envelopes in my pockets, and I wonder if there really is an angel keeping track of all the lying I'm doing without saying a word. If there is, my demerits are growing every week.

There's only one thing keeping me from going stark, staring mad with guilt at this point: the imminent return of Stevenston's very own star of stage and screen, Ellen Moon.

Allie is even more excited about Ellen coming home than me. We made a big poster board sign that read, "Welcome Home, Ellen!" We drew yellow stars to orbit around her name.

Today, we're going with Lindsey in her cherry red Chevy to bring Ellen home from the train station. Mrs. Moon would have liked to go with us, but somebody's got to look after Moon.

Mom helped Mrs. Moon with the baking. Between the two of them, they've got enough goodies to single-handedly supply the next community bake sale. Brownies and éclairs, crème puffs and raspberry tarts, pumpkin bread, and coconut cake.

The whole neighborhood smells like a bakery. Uncle Joe says he and Kate have each gained ten pounds just walking down our street! Kate gives him a good punch in the arm for that.

Lindsey stays in the car because the depot in Stevenston isn't exactly the best part of town, and she still wants to *have* a car after the train comes in. So, it's only Allie and me in the station to meet Ellen Moon.

I'm about to jump out of my skin, and Allie must feel the same because her feet can't seem to hold still. A voice comes over the PA system announcing the train from St. Louis. Allie and me each take one side of the big Welcome Home, Ellen!!! sign and head for the gate.

"Do you think Ellen is beautiful?"

"She's an actress from California," I say. "*Of course,* she's beautiful!"

Ellen's train approaches. The wheels squeal, and in the next two minutes, train doors open. Passengers start to unload.

Allie and me hold our sign and crane our necks, struggling to catch a first glimpse of Ellen Moon's glamorous self.

Two men in gray suits get off first. Then a dough-faced mom and three quarreling children struggle down the steps of the train. Then a sailor swaggers off, tipping his white hat to Allie and me. He sweeps up a girl into his arms and whirls her around.

"Brody's coming home by train," Allie gushes.

"Remind me to miss that homecoming."

We turn back to the emptying train, but that's it. No more passengers get off.

"Maybe she's having trouble with her luggage," Allie suggests.

We stand by the door and wait some more. Our starry welcome-home sign rides a little lower between us.

The announcer speaks into the PA system again. Passengers heading from Stevenston to Indianapolis and points east may now board the train.

Allie and me lower our sign.

"Maybe we got the time wrong," Allie says.

But we both know we didn't. We've been thinking of and planning for this for a whole week.

"Maybe she was kidnapped in St. Louis." I'm trying hard not to remember other broken promises. I want there to be a good reason she's not on that train.

"Maybe there's another train," Allie suggests.

"Yeah," I say. We walk to the ticket counter. But no, the clerk says there won't be another train from St. Louis until tomorrow.

We trudge back out to Lindsey's Chevy.

"Where's Ellen Moon?"

"She never got off the train," Allie tells her.

Lindsey drops her head on the steering wheel, "Oh, God, this is going to kill Mrs. Moon."

I slouched lower in the back seat, feeling meaner than sin, knowing I would be the one who has to tell her.

Lindsey pulls into the Moons' driveway, turns off her car, and we get out.

Mrs. Moon and Mom are standing on the front porch on either side of Moon. He is dressed to the nines in a new blue shirt and sharply creased pants. His white-fringed bald head shines in the October sun. The women wear wide smiles and peer past us at the empty Chevy.

"Mrs. Moon," I begin. I don't have to say anymore because I see she understands.

"Oh! I hope she isn't lost!"

As if Ellen were a three-year-old who'd strayed away in a department store. Then her free hand flies to her cheek. "Or hurt!"

Mom reaches past Moon to touch Mrs. Moon's shoulder. "I'm certain Ellen is fine. She probably missed a connection somewhere."

"Yes," Mrs. Moon says. "That must be it."

"I'll bet we'll be hearing from Ellen any minute," Mom goes on. "In the meantime ..."

And, as if Mom is some kind of conjurer, the Moons' telephone rings. Mrs. Moon hurries inside to answer it. The rest of us stand like sculptures frozen in place.

At last, Mrs. Moon opens the door and reappears on the front porch. "Good news, everyone! That was Ellen." her voice breaks a little. "She's okay. She landed a part in a commercial. So, she won't be coming back to Stevenston just yet."

"Oh!" Allie says, obviously impressed. She seems to have instantly forgiven Ellen in light of her towering success.

"Well," says Mom. "Fancy that! A television commercial!"

"Yes," says Mrs. Moon, sounding false and bright. "An *in-color* commercial."

"Maybe someone on the block will have a color TV set before Ellen's commercial airs." Mom suggests. "Won't that be something to see? Ellen Moon in living color!"

Moon tilts back his head and howls like a wounded hound.

"Come inside, Lenny, dear," Mrs. Moon pats his arm, cups his elbow, and leads him through the door. "All of you come inside. There's no sense letting delicious food go to waste."

The others troop inside. I plop down on the porch step and watch the sky burn down to evening. In a few minutes, I might be able to spot Venus rising over the horizon. I wonder if we'll ever fly there.

After a while, Allie comes out and sits beside me.

"Want a crème puff, Jessie?"

She hands me a pink glass plate filled with goodies and a rosebud-embroidered napkin. The napkins were from Mrs. Moon's wedding.

"Why aren't you eating?

"It takes four days to travel from California to Illinois by train," I say.

"Yeah, so?"

"So, for four days, Ellen Moon let Mrs. Moon and me and you, she let everyone in the neighborhood and even Uncle Joe and Kate believe she was coming home."

Allie has a little smudge of chocolate stuck to the corner of her mouth.

"She let us clean and bake and plan for her homecoming, and all the time, she knew it wouldn't happen. Doesn't that make you mad?"

"A little," Allie nods. "But it makes me happy, too."

"How could it make you happy?"

"Well," says Allie, snagging the bit of chocolate with her tongue. "Because it could have turned out a lot worse. What if Ellen really *was* kidnapped or hurt?"

"At least *then* she wouldn't be a jerk."

"Yeah, but people can stop being jerks," Allie says. "They can change their minds and be different. They can come home. But once they're really gone," Allie gazes at the darkening sky, "That's it. No second chances."

I think about Allie's real dad going out for cigarettes and about how Allie sees Brody differently than anyone else does. I figure maybe Allie's an expert at giving second chances.

"I guess that's true," I say.

"So, I'm happy. Besides, there's no point passing up a perfectly good party." She elbows me, "And Moon is asking for you."

"No, he isn't."

"You're right. He isn't," Allie grins. "But Mrs. Moon is."

"Well, in that case," I say. "Lead on."

Allie helps me to stand, and I follow her inside.

CHAPTER 21

November 22, 1963

I jab my fork into a wedge of lunchroom pecan pie and lift a bite to my mouth. Eddie has taken to sitting with a red-haired sophomore girl in the all-high school section of the cafeteria.

I don't care.

My science project is finished, except I'm waiting on a reply from the Russian embassy. I wrote to President Kennedy last week to ask him when he thought girls might be able to try out for astronaut training. Allie thinks that was a waste of good letter-writing paper. But then all Allie thinks about is Brody, Brody, Brody.

I'm about to be tired of it.

Allie leans closer to me and whisper-shouts in my ear, "I think our bunch should give Brody a welcome home party."

I roll my eyes. "We haven't had very good luck with welcome home parties if you remember. Besides, he'll already be having Thanksgiving with his family, won't he?"

Allie waves away the Beaman's turkey dinner and Ellen Moon's non-welcome home party with a sweep of her hand. "Not the same thing."

"Besides, if we give Brody a party, won't that be broadcasting your secret?"

"Not if YOU give the party."

"What?"

Sonny and Kevin plop their lunch trays down at our table.

"What're you two up to?"

"Planning a party," Allie trills.

"No, we're not!" I protest.

But Allie goes on. "For Brody. Jessie wants to have it in her basement."

I glare at her.

"Great! We haven't had a good knockdown drag-out fight since he left." Sonny says, pantomiming boxing with Kevin.

Allie punches Sonny's shoulder.

"Ow!" Sonny shakes his arm. "That's gonna leave a bruise."

Above us, the signal beep of the PA system sounds, and the principal's low steady voice comes on. But his words are just more background noise to be shouted over.

"Serves you right," Allie says. "Here's what we'll do. We'll all chip in for soda pop and snacks. I'll bring my records, and we'll have a sock hop in Jessie's basement."

Kevin rubs his chin, pretending to be deep in thought. "Think Brody learned how to Bunny Hop in boot camp?"

Allie rears back her fist to punch Kevin but stops mid-strike. She's staring up at the teachers' tables open-mouthed. I crane my neck to see what has her attention.

Mr. Tanner stands on top of the tables in the middle of the teachers' lunch trays. Turkey sandwiches and potato soup spill out from beneath his wingtip shoes. He's waving his arms, and his face is red with shouting.

"SHUT UP!" Mr. Tanner screams. "SHUT UP!"

Beside him, Miss. Martin covers her face with her hands: her shoulders tremble.

"WON'T YOU PLEASE SHUT UP?"

Gradually the deafening lunchtime din cycles down to a hum.

"Can't you people be quiet long enough to hear?" Mr. Tanner's voice catches. His arms fall to his sides. ***Can't you people be quiet long enough to hear? Your president has been shot!***

CHAPTER 22

November 25, 1963

I watch as much as I can stand of President Kennedy's funeral. When Jon Jon salutes his father's coffin and Allie's quiet crying turns to sobs, I have to get away from the TV.

Shrugging into last year's coat, I go outside into the bright fall day. I close the door on Allie's weeping and Mom's soft consolation. I feel as brittle as the November wind that lifts my hair and as cold.

My mind keeps playing a few words from President Kennedy's speech "We have tossed our hats over the wall of space…." I keep imagining the shiny stove-pipe black hat President Kennedy wore on his inaugural day, lifted from his head and blown clean away, out of reach on the raw November wind.

I make for my favorite thinking spot on our dwarf cherry tree. I climb up into its fruitless branches. I am utterly alone. I wait for something to happen, for someone to shake me awake from this terrible dream. But there is only the wind to keep me company.

After a while, Moon bangs out of his back door. He is coatless, but he wears a strange hat. He shuffles his way to a corner of the chain link fence. As he draws closer, I see the hat is the same one he wore in his wedding picture. It is his army hat from the Great War.

The hard November sun glitters on a star-shaped medal pinned to his chest pocket.

He grabs the corner fence post with both hands. Tips back his head and shouts to the sky, "NOOOOOOOO!" He holds his wail long and high, like an opera singer. He takes a breath. Then he tips back his head and begins again.

I do the same.

"NOOOOO! NOOOOO! NOOOOO! NOOOO! NOOOO!" Moon and me howl and howl and howl together until Mrs. Moon and Mom come to take us inside.

CHAPTER 23

Three More Days

I am nearly the last one to leave the school building. My grades have slipped this past month, and Miss. Martin kept me late to talk. It's past time to turn in my science project, but I cannot seem to finish it. It sits on a card table in my basement, still waiting for the waxed paper portholes to be fastened in and an aluminum foil heat shield added.

It is the project Miss. Martin says she is most excited about. I can't remember much more of the conversation. I know I must have promised to finish, but I can't think how I will manage it.

I push open the school doors and step outside. Snow swirls at my feet. For the past twenty-seven days, our flags have been flying at half–mast: the Stars and Stripes, our Illinois, and our school wildcat. They have been at half-mast since the day President Kennedy died.

I see them now snapping in the raw December wind and wonder if I will ever feel whole again.

Only three more days until the flags fly atop their poles again. Only three more days until our wounds begin to heal.

Only three more days until we can begin to forget.

I pull up the hood of my coat and trudge down the school walkway

I will never forget Caroline and Jon Jon watching their father's coffin pass. I will always remember Jon Jon's salute.

I wonder who we're kidding.

CHAPTER 24

Christmas Baskets

Our Christmas tree stands twinkling with light in the living room window. I open the door and breathe in familiar Christmas smells—pine and cinnamon, ginger, and cloves.

"Is that you, Jessie?" Mom calls from the kitchen.

"Yes," I call back.

Kate pokes her head into the dining room. She's been helping Mom with her wonderful Christmas baking.

"How's my junior maid of honor today?" Kate asks.

"Okay." I lie.

Uncle Joe and Kate settled on their marriage date. June 6th in the Veteran's Hall. Mom is Kate's Maid of Honor. I am Junior Maid of Honor. Brett is Ring Bearer. (I have a feeling that he might not be the best person for much responsibility). Dad is Best Man; Cal is Groom's Man. Uncle Joe says it will be good for Cal to practice walking down the aisle with Lindsey.

Mom and Kate are working on what sort of gowns we'll wear. I'm guessing there's time enough for that.

"If you're hungry, you may have a gingerbread man." Mom calls from the kitchen. "But take one of the broken ones. I'm saving the best ones for Christmas baskets."

I shrug out of my coat and throw it across the sofa back.

I choose a gingerbread man with only one arm. Kate stops my hand. She exchanges the broken man for a perfect one.

I bite its head off.

Kate munches the broken one.

There's a box on our dining room table wrapped up in brown paper addressed to PFC Brody Beaman, USMC. He served as part of the contingent of Marines lining the streets for President Kennedy's funeral.

Kate traces the address on the package.

"It's too bad he was only home for a week at Thanksgiving," Kate says. "I'm sure Allie was disappointed."

"Yes, she was."

I'm still playing courier pigeon. But mostly everyone knows about Allie and Brody. Except that is for Brody's folks. Now Brody has accepted a short time home in order to train for a special unit.

"Joe and I have been wondering." Kate begins. "If Allie might sing for us at our wedding?"

If Kate had asked me last summer, I'd say sure! But now….?

"Maybe you could ask her for me, Jessie?"

"I'll try."

Mom comes into the dining room. Her hair springs loose from the leather barrette. Her apron is sprinkled with flour.

"Oh, good, you found one," she says, smiling. "Does it taste all right?"

Kate offers Mom a bite of her broken one. Mom nips off one of the gingerbread man's feet. "Umm. We could have used a touch more molasses. But not bad overall."

Mom tucks a strand of hair behind her ear and eases herself into a dining room chair. She fingers the box of goodies for Brody.

"I hope I'm not too late in sending this." She frowns a little. "Probably Mr. Beaman will have sent his earlier, so Brody will still have a good Christmas."

I shrug. I don't think Old Man Beaman sent Brody anything for Christmas. But I'd bet Brody will be happy to get Mom and Kate's goodie box no matter when it comes.

"It'll be okay, Mattie." Kate picks another broken ginger man.

"Can you take Moons their Christmas basket?" Mom asks. "I'd like for them to have it early in case they have company."

"Sure," I say, even though Allie and me are the most company the Moons ever get.

Mom goes into the kitchen and returns with a basket decorated with red ribbon and covered with a gold-colored cloth. She hands the basket to me.

"I'll telephone Mrs. Moon to let her know you're coming."

And to see how Moon is behaving himself today, I think.

"You're really something, Jessie Chrisman," Kate says. "As strong as your mother."

I doubt that. But I don't say anything.

I walk to the living room and pull on my coat.

Mom finishes her conversation and hangs up the receiver. "She'll be watching for you."

I open the door and step onto the porch. More snow drifts now. Allie is just turning onto our walk.

"Oh!" Allie says, seeing the basket. "Are you leaving?"

"I'm taking the Moons, their Christmas basket," I say. "Want to come?"

"All right." Allie falls into step beside me. "No letter today?"

"Not today."

"Brody's doing really well," Allie says. "He's thinking about staying in the Marines even after his four-year hitch. He should make corporal by then, maybe even sergeant. He says that's pretty good pay."

"Why do you care how much money Brody makes?" I cock an eye at Allie. "What'd he do? Ask you to marry him?"

Allie shrugs. "We can't afford it yet."

I stop dead in the snow at the end of the Moon's walk. "Allie, you shouldn't even be *thinking* about marrying *anyone*."

"Why not? I'm almost fifteen," Allie says. "Lacy was sixteen when she married my dad."

And look how that turned out, I think. But what I say is, "What about singing, Allie? I thought you were going to Nashville and become a singing star."

"Oh, Jessie," Allie says. "That was just a big dream. I have as good of a chance at that as you do of…of going to the *moon!*"

I blink.

"Oh! You know what I *mean*." Allie touches my arm. "You might get to the moon—I hope you do. But me and singing— well, that's a fantasy, and the sooner I let go of it, the better."

"That's Hank talking."

Allie shakes her head. "No. It's me. I just don't *want* that anymore. It's too—*dangerous!* Too *iffy*. I need something more certain."

I stare at my friend.

"Listen, Jessie, can you keep a secret?"

"I can't believe you're asking me that. What do you think I've been doing all these weeks?"

"You're right," Allie says. "Sorry."

She slides her hand inside the collar of her coat and pulls out a gold chain. Dangling from the chain is a slender circle of gold with a tiny diamond in a raised setting. Allie slides the ring on the third finger of her left hand and turns it toward me.

"Where'd you get that?" I ask although I'm pretty sure I already know.

"Brody gave it to me when he was home," Allie says. "Isn't it beautiful? It's a promise ring."

"What did you promise?"

"To wait for each other," Allie says. "To be true."

I see Mrs. Moon's head in the little square of the door glass, peering out at us. She's ready to swing open her door and welcome us in.

"I can't talk about this anymore," I say. "Mrs. Moon is waiting."

"Okay," Allie says. "But I don't think I'll go in this time." She steps away from me and then turns back. "If I write Brody tonight, will you mail it tomorrow?"

I growl through my teeth. "Yes."

I watch my friend hurry up the sidewalk. The street lights flicker on in the gathering dark. Allie passes beneath one and turns to wave to me from a pale halo of light.

Her shadow falls gracefully behind her.

CHAPTER 25

Spit And Petrolatum Jelly

Mrs. Moon bundles me inside, and I hand her the Christmas basket.

"This is so lovely of you."

"Mom did it."

"Well, you braved the elements to bring it. That's nice, too." Mrs. Moon brushes snow from the shoulders of my coat. "Can you stay a bit? Lenny's napping, and I've made some cocoa."

"Yeah, I can stay."

"Wonderful! Take off your coat then, and make yourself at home," she says. "I'll be back in a jiffy."

I hang my coat on a hook by the Moons' front door and wander into their tiny living room. I cross to the bookcase and find her trio of pictures on the top shelf.

President Kennedy's picture has a wide length of black velvet ribbon draped across the frame. Stubby candles flicker in glass containers on either side. I look at his uplifted chin and his far-seeing eyes. Eyes that imagined a future that reached to the moon.

Now he's gone. I wonder how we'll even go on, let alone travel to the stars. The weight that settled in my chest twenty-seven days ago threatens to squeeze my heart into a tiny black cinder.

"Here we are, dear."

I turn and see her kind face through a blur of tears.

"Oh, Jessie!" Mrs. Moon sets down our cups of cocoa. She puts her arms around me and leads me to their lumpy sofa.

"There, now. Tell me all about it."

I shake my head. "I can't. You have enough to worry about…"

"Jessica Louise," Mrs. Moon says. "I'll thank you to let *me* decide what I can handle and what I can't!"

"Sorry," I blubber.

Mrs. Moon takes a handkerchief from her apron pocket and hands it to me. "Mop up and tell me what the trouble is."

I take the hankie and clean up.

"It's just," I begin, "I don't know! Everything seems so crazy. People getting shot for no good reason, leaving little kids to make out the best they can."

"President Kennedy?" Mrs. Moon says.

"Yeah."

"It is almost too sad to bear, isn't it?" Mrs. Moon smoothes my skirt over my knees. "Still, Caroline and Jon Jon have their mother. A braver woman than Jackie Kennedy I've never seen. I expect she'll see them through."

"I guess, but there are other things besides."

"What other things?"

"Like people giving up on dreams before they even get started. Just throwing them down like they never even mattered one bit.

Tromping on 'em." I grind my foot on the Moons' worn linoleum like I'm stomping an ant.

"Mmm," Mrs. Moon says. "Would that be you?"

"No! Well, maybe. I don't know. Everything seems so unpredictable. And so—*hard*!" I hunch my shoulders. "I could wake up one morning, and everything is one way, and before I go to bed, things are all turned upside down. You know, Mrs. Moon?"

Mrs. Moon tucks a strand of hair behind my ear. "Yes, dear, I do."

"It's so unfair!"

"That's true," Mrs. Moon agrees. "Every word."

Fat lot of help she is!

"Well then! What's to keep the world from flying apart?" I explode my fingers in front of Mrs. Moon's face. "Boom! Just like that? Disintegrated! In one big atomic flash!"

Mrs. Moon draws back, surprised, blinking.

"SPIT and PETROLEUM JELLY," Moon booms from a bedroom archway.

Mrs. Moon and I look up.

"Try that for sticking together," says Moon, scratching his head. "Works wonders."

Mrs. Moon pats my hands and rises to greet her husband.

"Lenny, dear, we're having cocoa. Would you like some? We have peppermint sticks for stirring…"

Mrs. Moon leads her husband to the dining room table and sits him down with one of Mom's perfect gingerbread men.

Having cocoa and cookies with Moon is quite an adventure. He's silent most of the time, only joining in the conversation when he has something profound to draw our attention to, like a procession of dragonflies jitterbugging across the dining room window.

"I expect the Christmas lights are fooling you, Lenny, dear." Mrs. Moon says to that particular observation. But Moon remains unconvinced.

At a quarter past five, Mom telephones and asks Mrs. Moon to send me home for supper.

I take down my coat from the hook and slide my arms inside.

"I've been terribly selfish, keeping you so long from home, Jessie," Mrs. Moon says. "If you can stay one more minute, I have something for you."

Mrs. Moon rummages beneath her Christmas tree and brings out a large square box wrapped in blue and silver paper.

"This is for you, Jessie," she says, beaming. "From Lenny and me."

"But I didn't buy you anything!"

"Tut-tut, dear, you give us a gift every time you visit."

I shake the box gently and hear something shift inside. "What is it?" I ask.

"Mustard gas," Moon says.

Mrs. Moon smothers a laugh with her hand. "I promise you, Jessie, it is *not* mustard gas." She opens the front door, and I step onto her porch.

"Thank you for the cocoa and the present."

"You are most welcome, Jessie," Mrs. Moon says. Then putting one arm around my shoulders, she whispers. "It's us, who'll keep the world from flying apart," she says. "You and me and your mother and you're Uncle Joe and Kate. And millions of other ordinary folks all over the world looking after each other the best we can."

Mrs. Moon's hair shines white in the December night. "We're the ones who will hold it all together."

I whisper, "Please, God, let her be right."

CHAPTER 26

June 8, 1964

Allie stands by my dresser, spinning the star globe the Moons gave me last Christmas. Constellations whirl beneath her hands.

Next to the star globe stand my Friendship 7 and Vostok 6 models, and above them, taped to the wall, is an autographed picture of Lt. Col. John Glenn, the first American to orbit the Earth. A blue ribbon is thumb-tacked next to his picture. I never did get a picture of Valentina Tereshkova except for the ones I cut out from the newspapers, but they're on the wall too.

"Do you honestly think I was okay?" Allie asks for about the zillionth time.

"You were amazing, Allie. Everyone said so."

My Uncle Joe and Kate were married last Saturday, and Allie sang at their wedding in front of fifty people. While she sang, not a person stirred. No one even coughed. That's how good she was.

"I think they paid me too much."

We've covered this ground before, too. "Nope. Kate says twenty dollars is absolutely the going rate for wedding singers in 1964."

"Well," Allie says. And she spins the star globe again.

"Uncle Joe says once you've been paid for something, that automatically makes you a professional," I add. "You'd be silly to stop now. Nashville isn't that far away."

Allie slides the promise ring back and forth on its chain. "I wish Brody could have been here."

"Um hmm," I say, "I scoop a scrim of Petroleum jelly from the jar by my bed and rub it into my ball glove.

"Hey, you guys!" Kevin calls to us, his face pressed flat against my bedroom window screen. "You playin' baseball or not?"

"Yeah, hurry up before I gotta shave," Blinks says.

"We're coming. Hold your horses!" I shout back.

"Okay, but Eddie and me already picked," Kevin informs us. "Eddie gets you, Jessie, and I took Allie."

Our friends' faces disappear from the window.

Allie sighs. "Just once, I wish we could play on the same team."

"Yeah, me too," I say, taking off my bulky oxfords and sliding into my sneakers. "But even if that never happens, we'll always be a pair. No matter what."

Allie smiles.

She spits on her pinky finger, and I do the same.

We hook our fingers together and pull.

Friends forever. We swear it.

Author Bio

Ruth Siburt lives in Central Illinois where she spoils her beautiful, smart, loving grandchildren. She enjoys reading and writing stories, poetry, and sometimes her songs. She is a fan of children, cats, dogs, and birds. (Please don't hold the cat thing against her.)

She learned storytelling in two ways: through reading books and listening to her mom, Beulah. At our Sunday dinner table, Beulah told true stories from her childhood. She remembered what life was like living with relatives who gave her temporary homes. Ruth learned how stories come to life by paying attention to special moments. She works hard to remember them so she can share her stories with others.

Young Ruth dreamed of becoming a ballerina. Her parents decided to give her piano lessons instead. It turns out that was a smart choice. Ruth's fingers are much nimbler than her toes. She discovered in her piano lessons a sweet pairing of music and words. This is a good thing to know. She hopes her readers enjoy the wedding of music and story in Spoon Song.

Books by Ruth Siburt

Dragon Charmer: In the year 2080 thirteen-year-old Cady's life has been almost unbearable. Her father died the winter before. So, now it's Cady who looks after her 4-year-old sister, Sara, and their mother. The only comfort Cady has is her love for those mystical beasts Dragons. Cady is so taken with them that she sometimes feels as if she can hear them singing. Then, one day while Cady's mom and sister are busy with library story time Cady meets a remarkable person—a silver-haired, elderly woman who claims to be a dragon charmer. That woman is searching for the next charmer to take over the care and feeding of one of the last living dragons on Earth. Cady is the top candidate for the dragon's next charmer.

The Trouble with Alex: It was supposed to be the best summer of fourteen-year-old Kelly Lathrop's life. That was until her 9-year-old cousin Alex came to spend the summer. "I don't babysit." Alex reminded her mom. But it didn't matter Alex was coming for the duration. What none of them realized was Alex had a plan of his own. A fire-cracker plan if there ever was one. (This book is out of circulation.)

Spoon Song: My rhyming picture book from Words Matter Publishing. A young girl longs to find her place in her family's annual reunion festivities.